PRAISE FOR
Caleb and Kit

"A realistic story with strong, recognizable characters that doesn't reduce cystic fibrosis to a tragedy."

—*Kirkus Reviews*

"A can't-put-it-down tale. Caleb's discoveries about his own strength and resilience during his friendship with free-spirited, imaginative Kit will expand your heart and fill your soul. From the beautiful cover to the last sentence, this book is a favorite to savor and share."

—**Bibi Belford,**
author of *Canned and Crushed*

"You can't help but fall in love with twelve-year-old Caleb, his humor, his determination, and his wonder as he navigates his friendship with the mysterious Kit, his changing school relationships, his divorced parents' issues, and his comparisons to his big brother. You cry and cheer as he learns how hard it can be to do the right thing."

—**Tricia Clasen,**
author of *The Haunted House Project*

"Having a disability myself, my heart broke for Caleb, who wants nothing more than to feel like a normal twelve-year-old kid—at any cost. Caleb and Kit will forever be entwined, the roots of their friendship solid, rich, and strong, just like this beautiful story."

—**Kerry O'Malley Cerra,**
author of *Just a Drop of Water*

"In the midst of Kit's self-constructed fantasy world, Caleb's heroism is the real deal. He's determined, courageous, and witty despite his unusual physical challenges. Beth Vrabel doesn't shy away from the tough stuff that can complicate the lives of tweens. Readers young and old will find this a unique novel well-deserving of a permanent place on the family bookshelf."

—**Melissa Hart,**
author of *Avenging the Owl*

PRAISE FOR
ᏴETH ᏤRABEL

"Vrabel takes three knotty, seemingly disparate problems—
bullying, the plight of wolves, and coping with disability—and
with tact and grace knits them into an engrossing
whole of despair and redemption."

—*Kirkus Reviews*, **starred review**

"Vrabel displays a canny understanding of
middle-school vulnerability."

—*Booklist*

"[Vrabel's] challenging subject matter is handled in a gentle,
age-appropriate way with humor and genuine affection."

—*School Library Journal*

"Vrabel tackles some tough issues, including albinism,
depression, and loneliness, with a compassionate
perspective and a charming voice."

—**Amanda Flower,**
author of Agatha Award-winning Andi Boggs series

"Beth Vrabel's stellar writing captivates readers from the start
as she weaves a powerful story of friendship and hardship."

—**Buffy Andrews,**
author of *The Lion Awakens* and *Freaky Frank*

CALEB and KIT

CALEB and KIT

~>>>>> <<<<~

Beth Vrabel

Author of the Pack of Dorks series

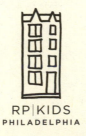

RP|KIDS
PHILADELPHIA

Running Press Kids
Hachette Book Group
1290 Avenue of the Americas, New York, NY 10104
www.runningpress.com/rpkids
@Running_Press

Printed in the United States of America

First Edition: September 2017

Published by Running Press Kids, an imprint of Perseus Books, LLC,
a subsidiary of Hachette Book Group, Inc.

The Hachette Speakers Bureau provides a wide range of authors for speaking events.
To find out more, go to www.hachettespeakersbureau.com or call (866) 376-6591.

The publisher is not responsible for websites (or their content)
that are not owned by the publisher.

Print book cover and interior design by Frances J. Soo Ping Chow

Library of Congress Control Number: 2016953715

ISBNs: 978-0-7624-6223-0 (hardcover), 978-0-7624-6224-7 (ebook)

LSC-C

10   9   8   7   6   5   4   3   2   1

FOR

WILL, JACK, AND JOEY

CHAPTER ONE

Kit said we were destined to meet, but I really was just going for a walk.

I had to get out of the house and away from my brother, who was sawing on his violin so hard that the noise seemed to vibrate up through my chest and out of my ears. Maybe he was just practicing, but then again, maybe my perfect brother was showcasing yet another way he was better than me. Back went the bow. *Look at what I'm doing while you just sit there!* Forward. *When I was twelve, I'd already performed concertos.* Back. *I'm captain of the cross-country team, but you can't even run a mile.* Forward, entering the cadenza. *Pathetic!* Back. *Loser!* Forward. *Lazy!*

Not that Patrick would actually say any of those things. He was too polite, too considerate, too *perfect* for that.

I had to leave. I grabbed my backpack and shouted over my shoulder, "Going for a walk!"

I thought Patrick wouldn't be able to hear me, but I suppose I had to add super-hearing to my big brother's long, long, *long* list of skills.

"Some exercise is a good idea, Caleb!" he hollered, now easing back into the concerto's slow ending. "Don't overdo it. Bring your—"

The door slammed behind me before he could finish. Patrick always acted like he was my parent just because he's five years older than me. The music stopped before I got to the end of the driveway, and the door flew open again with a bang.

Patrick stood there with his violin in hand. "Wait! Caleb, I'll go—"

Before Patrick could finish his offer to come along, I quickened my pace and ducked from the driveway, even though that meant plunging right into the woods that border our house. I knew Patrick would put away his violin carefully and exactly before following me, but that only gave me a couple seconds' head start, so I had to act fast. I jumped over a fallen log. Briars scraped the sliver of skin between my socks and my pant leg, but I plunged ahead anyway.

I hardly ever went into the woods surrounding our house. Brad, my best friend, usually came by on his bike, and we'd stick to the cul-de-sac, playing pickup when I felt up to it, H.O.R.S.E. when I didn't. We used to race in electric go-karts. Mom still kept them charging in the garage, just in case Brad decided they weren't too babyish anymore now that we were twelve. Part of me thought he said they were babyish because I was so much better at drifting than he was, and he didn't know how to handle being slower than me.

But Brad wasn't around much now that he had both baseball and football practices.

Once the woods were thick around me, I figured Patrick would have given up on finding me and retreated back into the house. I looked up to the branches of the huge trees above me. Two long, thick trunks soared straight to the sky and then curved away from each other. I had heard once about trees that do that—live side by side but bend away to share the sun. They are buddies. They could stick close, but if they do, eventually one will struggle to tower over the other, keeping the weaker, unluckier one in the shade. Instead, if they are *really* friends, they'll bend apart. I wondered if it hurt, twisting away from your friend like that.

I squinted, and for a second the branches looked like the inside of a pair of lungs, stretching in all directions from the trunk, always reaching for more, more, more.

My own lungs ballooned as a breeze rustled through the trees' leaves. Hoping I wouldn't get lost, I went deeper into the thicket. Here's the thing: I live in a small neighborhood. It wasn't like these woods would stretch for miles. A couple acres, maybe, tops. Other people's houses bordered the thick circle of trees like mine, so the worst that could happen was that I'd end up across the woods in someone's backyard.

That was what I told myself anyway. I yanked the backpack strap up my shoulder and unzipped the front compartment, making sure my inhaler was there. It wouldn't buy me a lot of time, but it was better than nothing.

I decided the best direction to head was straight back. If I stayed on the path I'd forged, then all I'd have to do to find my way home was turn around, right? Yeah, I guess that's why I'd never make it as a Boy Scout. Of course as soon as I couldn't see my house anymore, that's when the trees got all squished together like bullies, totally zapping the chance of my walking in a straight line. I stepped over broken branches, around trunks, through prickly bushes. There was no way I'd find my way back now by just turning around.

Each step I took made my shoes suck deeper into mud with a squelching sound, and each time I lifted my feet it made my chest hurt. A few more yards in and I realized I was in trouble. My chest *burned.* I tried to ignore it. The pain twisted and coiled around my ribs—not like I couldn't breathe but like my body didn't want to. Like I was drowning from the inside out. I tried not to think about how fast my heart was beating and only that totally freaking out was useless. I tried not to croak out a cry or anything babyish like that. This wasn't my first panic attack; I knew I wasn't really dying. But every time it happened, I had to convince myself all over again. And the attacks had been happening more and more.

I tried to focus on what was going on around me. Sunlight trickled through the thick woods. Maybe there was a clearing? The opening was also the reason for the gross mud I was plodding through. Just inside the clearing there was a stream that cut through the woods. The stream was shallow, only a couple inches deep, but wide, stretching as far as my yard. Sunshine glinted off the water, where it trickled over stones the size of my fist and around large boulders.

I'm not dying, I told myself over and over. *I'm not dying*. It was just a panic attack.

I'm okay. I fell to my knees, not caring when they sank into the mud, drenching my pant legs with thick dark muck. Leaning forward, I plunged my palms into the cool water. *I'm okay*. The smooth, cold rocks seemed to be pressing back as much as my hands pushed against them. *I'm okay*.

The slow lap of water over my skin helped me focus. I concentrated on what Mom had told me to do when I got like this—count out my breaths, make sure the exhales matched the inhales, try to make each last a count of three, then four, then five. *Five is fine*, she always said. *When you get to five, you know you're okay*. What she meant was: if I could stretch out each breath to five seconds, then it was just my head that was convinced I was dying. Not my lungs. Still, I thought about my inhaler, zipped in the front pocket of my backpack. Was it time to grab it?

I held off, breathing in and out instead, counting. Like usual, Mom was right. I flexed my fingers in the water, noticing for the first time the minnows racing around the stones and the sudden flush of swirling mud when a crawfish hid beneath a loose rock.

Even though I felt better (relief over not actually dying sort of washed away the whole lost-in-the-woods worry for the moment), I stayed put, searching for the bluish-gray crawfish in the settling water. It only took a few seconds for me to spot it creeping along, its oversize pinchers outstretched. Quick as I could, I plunged my fingers into the stream to catch it. Its tail sent a swish of water between my fingers as it dashed away.

"You've got to be a lot faster than that."

The voice above made me jerk, sending my already drenched knees slipping into the water. This time the voice laughed—a tinkling sound.

I rose to my feet, face burning, and squinted into the sunlit clearing to see who was talking. A huge boulder sat in the middle of the stream. And on top of it, her legs folded neatly beside her, perched an angel.

Stupid thought, right? But I swear, the sun shone straight on her, making the top of her dark brown hair glimmer like a halo and the yellowish boulder upon which she sat shine like gold. Oh, man. Had I been wrong? Maybe it hadn't been a panic attack. Maybe I *had* died!

The girl laughed again and slid down to land barefoot in the water with a quick splash. She walked toward me with a wide smile and her hands folded behind her back. "I've gotten really good at catching them," she said. "You've got to put one hand behind them, and then, with your other hand, splash the water in front of them. They'll fly right back into your first hand."

"Oh," I mumbled, my face flaming. "How—how long have you been here?"

The girl's bottom lip jutted out for a moment and she looked up toward the sun as if doing math in her head. Her eyes were pale blue like a patch of sky behind puffy clouds. Freckles sprinkled across her nose and cheeks. "Maybe an hour or so," she said. "I'm trying to catch a bird, but they all keep ignoring me, even when I whistle at them."

"A bird? Why?"

"Well," the girl said as she smoothed her hands on her ratty white sundress, "I've figured out how to catch the crawfish and the minnows. Seems like birds would be next."

The corner of my mouth jerked upward. "Quit messing around." But even as I said it a dark crow swooped overhead.

The girl shrugged her narrow shoulders, and I knew she hadn't been joking.

"You really want to catch a bird?"

The girl nodded.

"Why?"

"Why not?" She smiled again. I guess I was still making sure she was real, because my brain seemed to pick up on things about her that I don't usually notice with other people. Things like how her chin was small but pointed, how one of her front teeth slanted over the other, how her eyelashes captured sunlight as much as her hair. It made remembering to talk take longer than it should have.

"Because . . . ," I managed because I was apparently an amazing conversationalist.

"Because . . . ," she repeated.

"Because . . . what would you do with it once you had it?"

The girl's smile stretched wider. "I haven't thought that far ahead yet." She jerked out her hand to shake like we were parents meeting in the school parking lot instead of two kids standing in a stream. "I'm Kit. I live here."

"Here? In the water?"

She laughed again, but not in a mean way. "Of course not, silly. I live in a house that way." She jerked her thumb over her shoulder toward the other side of the stream. "And you?"

"Oh." I smoothed my wet palm against a dry part of my pants and shook her hand. It was warm, probably from the sun-drenched rock she had been sitting on. "I'm Caleb. I live that way." I nodded my head backward. "At least I think I do. I'm sort of lost."

"Awesome," Kit said. You know how people talk about eyes sparkling? I always thought that was just a stupid thing people said when they meant someone looked happy. But it's not, because Kit's eyes could do that. They sparkled. If she were a comic book character, a little *ding* would be written in curly letters over her eyes. "Getting lost means you get to have an adventure." She stepped backward into the stream, her eyes steady on mine like a dare. "Are you ready?"

I didn't normally do this kind of thing—follow random girls deep into the woods, I mean. But I didn't even have to think this time. I just kicked off my sneakers and tossed them onto the bank. "Ready." I followed her across the stream.

⇥〉〉〉.〈〈〈⇤

Kit led me along a narrow trail deeper into the woods. She stopped suddenly, and I bumped into her. "Look!" She pointed to long, skinny blossoms hanging from weeds growing along the path. The flowers looked like tiny trumpets. "Honeysuckles!" She plucked a blossom and peeled back the petals. Then she popped the middle into her mouth.

"Try one." She handed me a blossom. Her fingernails were brown, probably from catching so many crawfish in the mud.

"Are you sure you know what these are?"

Kit didn't answer, just peeled another flower. I sniffed at the blossom. It smelled like honey but, when I put the edge on my tongue, it tasted more like perfume.

"How old are you, anyway?" Kit asked, an eyebrow raised as she studied my face.

I lifted my chin, threw my chest out. "I'm twelve."

That eyebrow popped up a smidge higher. I knew why. I didn't look like a twelve-year-old. I was sort of like Chris Evans at the beginning of the first Captain America movie—the part before the scientist gave Steve Rogers the elixir of super serum and he was just frail looking and scrawny. I'm too short and way too skinny for my age. I'm so used to the air fighting its way out of me that sometimes I forget to close my mouth when I breathe; Patrick says it makes me look like a toddler with my stomach puffed out and mouth hanging open. My brown hair is long, I guess, and it flops on my head instead of lying flat and smooth like Brad's or waving back over my head like Captain America's. Also not helping me in the looking-my-age department are my huge brown eyes; they're the reason Patrick used to call me Bambi—that is, until Mom grounded him from playing his violin for a weekend when I made a huge fuss about it.

I braced myself for Kit to do what everyone else did when they found out how old I was—saying something like, "What? I thought you were nine!" or "No way! My baby sister is bigger than you!"

But Kit didn't say any of that. Her grin widened, and her eyebrow lowered. "Cool. Me, too."

➤➤➤ ⫷⫷⫷

Kit's house was about as opposite of my own plain red brick home as it could get. The house stood at least three stories, and I counted just as many chimneys poking up from the dark green roof. Tons of narrow windows with swirling thin wood trim at the top, like icing on a cupcake, marched up the sides of the white structure. At least, it had been white once. Now it was mostly gray, with long strips of peeling paint curling on the sides. The ceilings of the three balconies that popped out of the sides of the Victorian mansion were painted green to match the roof. It looked like a regular boxy house that someone had added on to, with rooms and porches jutting out in angles. The twisting spokes of the balcony rails were painted in pink and blue, making me think of the gingerbread house Hansel and Gretel had stumbled upon in the woods. Once, I could tell, it had looked amazing. It still did, but in a faded sort of way. "You live here?" I asked.

"Yeah," said Kit, shielding her face from the sun with her hand as we looked up at a turret with windows all around that jutted out from the top. Kit pointed to it. "That's my room."

"Isn't it too bright?" I asked.

"I like the sun."

"Of course," I said without thinking.

"What do you mean?" Kit lowered her eyes to meet mine, and my face flamed again.

I shrugged instead of answering. How was I supposed to say *Of course you like the sun, you* are *a sun* without feeling like a dork? But when Kit's mouth twitched into a smile I somehow knew she had read my mind.

"So how come I haven't seen you at school?" I asked.

"Because I've never been to school."

"Ever?"

"Well, not since kindergarten, anyway. It just didn't work out. You know, teachers telling me what to do, how to behave, how to share and take turns." Kit rolled her eyes. I laughed.

"Yeah," I said, "the whole standing-in-line thing about did me in, too."

Kit raised her fist. "I had to take a stand! Mom homeschools me."

I shuddered. For a while, back when I was in fourth grade, my mom had to homeschool me after I was in the hospital for a long time. We both hated it. Her voice would go all hard and fake-happy when I didn't understand something or when she did a math problem in a confusing way. "That stinks."

"Not really." Kit shrugged. "I can study whatever I want. Or nothing at all."

My head jerked back at the thought. Every day that Mom homeschooled me, she had a plan and *so many lists*. Thinking about Mom made me wonder how long I had been gone. I went up on my tiptoes, trying to figure out which direction led to my house.

Kit's house's dirt driveway led to a wooded road, and woods surrounded the house in all directions. I couldn't figure out which way led to the main drag back toward my house. "Do you mind if I use your phone? I left my cell at home, and my brother's going to go nuts if he doesn't hear from me soon."

"Yes," Kit said.

"Excuse me?"

"Yes, I mind." She sat down on the wide front-porch steps and hummed a little.

"Why?"

"We don't have a phone," she said serenely.

"No phone?"

"No phone." A skinny cat crawled out from under the porch and curled between my legs. It climbed the porch steps and darted around Kit to disappear into the house. Kit hummed. "Not yet, anyway. We just moved in a couple weeks ago. This was Grandmom Ophelia's house, but she died last month. Mom and I are living here, taking over the estate."

"But you don't have a phone?"

"Not yet," Kit said, still humming.

"How do you keep in touch with people?"

Kit shrugged. "Mom has a phone but she keeps it with her."

My mouth opened and closed a couple times. "What if you need help?"

"Why would I need help?" she asked.

For just a second my chest caught fire again. I swallowed it back so I could think. "What if something happened?"

"Then I'd deal with it."

I shook my head. "Can I borrow your mom's phone, then?"

Kit leaned back on her elbows. "She isn't here."

"When is she getting back?"

"I have no idea." Kit stood and brushed the peeled paint flecks from the porch stoop off her dress. She sighed and rolled her eyes. "Listen, if it's a big deal, I'll show you how to get home."

"I'm sorry," I muttered. But the simmering in my chest settled.

"Next time, bring your phone so you can stay longer. This doesn't even count as an adventure." Kit skipped a little as she turned back toward the woods.

"I will," I said, feeling stupid as I trailed behind her but also kind of happy since she had said "next time."

"Can you come here tomorrow?"

Man, I was glad I was behind Kit so she didn't see the huge grin that spread across my face. "Yeah, after school."

"Or . . . you could skip school and meet me on the golden boulder. It's a perfect breakfast spot." Kit held back a stray branch so it wouldn't smack me in the face. "The fairies sweep it clean every morning at dawn." I fake-laughed, but Kit just stared at me like the fairy thing wasn't a joke at all.

I coughed into my elbow. "Wouldn't your mom get a little suspicious if she suddenly had another student to homeschool?"

Kit's eyebrows sunk but she just shrugged. "I think I'm going to take tomorrow off."

"You can do that?" I asked. "Just decide to take the day off?"

"I can do whatever I want," she said.

"Well, we only have two more days of school," I said, but Kit didn't answer. Not that I was super excited about school ending or anything. This summer was going to be the worst ever, thanks to the stupid day camp Mom was forcing me to go to. "Do you stop school for the summer?"

Kit shrugged. "I guess we will."

At the edge of the stream, I paused before stepping in, not sure if the rocks would be slippery. Kit leaped from smooth rock to smooth rock. The beams of sunlight through the breaks in the trees' canopies were like a spotlight on her steps, like I was following a yellow brick road. *Where would it lead?* I wondered as I placed one foot into the stream.

CHAPTER TWO

The whir of the air conditioner made it tough to tune in to Mrs. Richards as she went over details of our end-of-the-year essay. A master of creativity, Mrs. Richards decided this year's theme would be "How I Plan to Spend My Summer."

All around me, kids leaned toward the chilly air as it pumped out of the air conditioner. That is, everyone but Shelly Markel, who pulled on a cardigan and held on to her bony elbows like she was icing over.

"It's so, so cold!" she whined when Mrs. Richards answered her half-raised hand. Shelly gripped her elbows again and, between chattering teeth, said, "It's only eighty degrees out! Can't we just have the windows open like *every other room*?"

Mrs. Richards's eyes slid to me and then to the floor. "No, the air-conditioning is important to . . . to cutting back the humidity. We're very lucky to have it!"

The rest of the school wasn't air-conditioned. Just my classroom. Just for me. As if on cue, a cough rippled up and out of me. I wiped at my mouth with a tissue. Shelly scrunched her nose and shuddered, this time not at the cold.

"But it's *so* uncomfortable!" she whined.

Mrs. Richards smiled. "Think how good it's going to feel when you come back from recess!"

"Ugh!" Shelly sighed. Her lips did look a little blue, I guess. It was hard to tell since they were pressed together so tightly. Her ponytail jiggled a little from her shivering so hard. Or, at least, her *acting* like she was shivering so hard.

"Shut it, Shelly," Brad hissed when Mrs. Richards turned back to the front of room. He yanked on her ponytail, then crossed his arms behind his head and tilted toward the cold air. Brad grinned at me.

I shook my head and scribbled *How I Plan to Spend My Summer* across the top of my notebook page like Mrs. Richards had asked.

"Now," the teacher said, "jot down a few ideas below that."

Shelly's pencil scratched out idea after idea. Behind her, Brad muttered to himself, "Football practice, dirt bikes, water skiing . . ."

But I only came up with two words.

"What kit?" Brad asked when the bell rang a minute later. He was leaning over my shoulder.

"What?" I asked, jamming the notebook page into my folder.

"Your summer plans." He sat on the edge of Shelly's desk, effectively trapping her in her seat. She zipped her backpack harder than necessary and sighed deeply but didn't say anything, just like he knew she wouldn't. Shelly's been in the same class as me and Brad since kindergarten and had yet to say a single word to him. Her face flushed the color of a ripe red garden tomato whenever she looked his way, though.

Brad ignored her grumbling or maybe truly didn't notice her. I never could tell. "Your essay. All you wrote down was 'With Kit.' With what kit? Is it another model superhero thing?"

I shrugged. "Nothing, I just—I just couldn't come up with anything." For some reason, I hadn't mentioned meeting Kit to Brad. Not because I was hiding anything. It just hadn't come up. I mean, I guess it was coming up now, but something kept me from saying anything. Part of me wondered if I hadn't imagined the whole thing—going off on my own, finding a girl in the water, seeing her mansion hidden in the woods. It sounded more like a fairy tale than a real life thing.

And, yeah, okay, part of me—a big part—knew that if Kit met Brad I'd go from being Caleb to being "Brad's friend Caleb" almost instantly. That's always what happened. It wasn't Brad's fault or anything. He was a great friend. My *best* friend, since forever. But somehow he seemed to suck up all the oxygen in any room he was in. Everyone else just sort of existed around him. Instead of Caleb and Kit, we'd become Brad and Kit with me in parentheses at the end.

Brad tossed a football casually in the air, making it twirl as it landed back in his hands. "Ready to play?"

"Yeah, you bet!" I said. Brad clapped his hand on my shoulder as I zipped up my backpack and stood.

"I don't get why you need a special air conditioner but can play football at recess," Shelly snapped behind us.

Without turning around, Brad and I said, "Shut it, Shelly," at the same time.

⤙❯❯❯❭ ❬❬❬❬⤚

As we headed out the metal double doors to the recess area, Brad tossed the ball to me and ran backward, hands up, for me to throw it to him. Back and forth we threw the ball until we got to the open field where a dozen other guys were already gathered. "All right," said Brad, tucking the ball under his arm after divvying people up for teams. "Ready?"

"Wait a sec!" Jett, a kid who had just joined the football team, held up his hands. "Your side has an extra player. That's not fair."

"It's just Caleb," Jack, Jett's team captain, said, then stiffened when a crumpled-up sort of noise leaked out of me.

"But why do they get an extra player?" Jett pressed.

Brad popped him in the shoulder with the heel of his hand. "Lay off."

We ran to our huddle, though the soupy air was already making it a little harder than it should've been for me to hustle.

"Here's how it's going to go," Brad said. "We're doing a counter. I'm going to fake to Ian, so you head right. I'll hand off to Caleb."

"No, man!" I said. The other guys around us didn't say anything. Still, I could see they were annoyed.

Brad grinned, making the dimple in his cheek flash. "I'm telling you, it'll work. I'll pass the ball right into your hands. All you've got to do is barrel down the middle. Zach, Logan, you guys make a path for him. Cool?"

Reluctantly, I nodded. The other guys did, too.

Brad slammed his hand down on my shoulder again. "They'll never expect it!"

"Because it'll never work," Zach muttered when Brad jogged off to the field.

I went to my usual spot in the backfield. Brad turned and nodded at me before stooping to take the pass off. He was totally confident that I could do this. And you know what? For a second I believed him.

Ian charged ahead and Brad arced his arm, ready to launch the ball toward him. Guys on the other team darted in Ian's direction. Everyone but Jett, whose eyes locked on the ball still clutched in Brad's hand. But it was too late to back out now, even as Jett rushed in my direction, even as Brad rammed the ball into my hands.

I ran ahead, pumping my legs. I tried to swivel around Jett, but there was no stopping him. He barreled right into me, hurling me in the air to land with a *slam* onto my back.

"Yeah!" Jett cheered, but everyone else was silent. That is, until Brad rammed into him, knocking Jett to the ground beside where I now hacked into my fist, coughing up sticky phlegm and mucus.

"What's wrong with you?" Brad shouted.

"I'm sorry!" I coughed. "He's just fast!"

But Brad wasn't yelling at me. Instead he was hollering in Jett's face. "What's your problem?"

"My problem?" Jett hopped to his feet. "I'm playing the game! Why is he playing if you're going to freak when he gets knocked?"

"It's all right!" I pushed myself up, still coughing. "It's fine." I tried to smile but it came out wobbly. "He did me a favor, actually, breaking up some of the gunk in my lungs."

But Brad's face still flamed. His hands were still curled into fists. "Why'd you tackle him?"

"It's football," Jett countered.

"It's *Caleb*," Brad spit back.

Instantly I was ice-water cold. I stepped back. Twice. Then I turned and strode off the field.

"Hold up!" Brad yelled at my back. "Hang on, Caleb. I didn't mean it like that. I'm sorry. *I'm sorry!*"

I shook my head, not bothering to turn around. Brad's quick foot-steps crunched the dry grass as he ran to catch up to me. "I didn't mean it like that," he said, his voice dropping.

"I know." I shrugged, fighting to keep my voice neutral. "Always wondered why no one ever tackled me."

Brad didn't say anything. He just breathed out long and slow when I stopped striding off the field. "It's not like it's a rule or anything," Brad said. "The guys, we just try not to knock you around too much."

My eyes burned but I wasn't crying or anything. "Right," I said.

"Come on." Brad's arm raised to slam down on my shoulder. Without thinking, I dodged him. "Let's go back."

"No, man," I said. "I'm good."

Brad stopped walking but I didn't. "You can keep score or some-thing," he called to my back. But I just kept walking away.

"Caleb?" Mrs. Richards asked as I walked past. "Would you like to come inside with me? It's a little hot out here."

"No, thanks. I'm fine."

"I'd love your company," she said.

I shook my head and kept going, sitting so my back was pressed against the brick of the school wall and a shadow covered me like a cool blanket.

"Awww . . . did you get knocked down by the big bad football player?" Shelly suddenly stood in front me, her arms crossed and voice singsongy like she was talking to a baby.

"Leave me alone, Shelly."

"Sucks not getting special treatment for once, doesn't it," she said, and turned on her heel to walk away.

Anger surged through me, enough so that I probably could've scooped it up and thrown it to splatter across her like a water balloon. But I fisted a handful of dry grass instead, yanking it from the hard ground and crushing it between my fingers.

—⟫⟫⟫⟨⟨⟨⟨—

"What's your deal?" Brad charged up to where I sat at lunch. He peered around the table, seeing backpacks claiming all the seats around me. He nabbed one and pulled it from the chair, chucking it onto the table behind us.

"I think someone was going to sit there," I pointed out as I unpacked my lunch box. I never bought lunch like Brad and the rest of the guys, and I usually got to the cafeteria before anyone else, since I had to swing by the nurse's office for a nebulizer treatment and six or seven Creon tablets before I ate. I was glad to be early most days, though. Getting a seat at the right table in the cafeteria was all strategy—come in quick as you can, dump your bag to save your seat, and then hop into line before someone cooler than you came along and moved your bag.

"It's just Zach." Brad shrugged and slunk into the seat. My eyes slid to the lunch line where Zach waited. His hands curled into fists, but I knew he wouldn't say anything to Brad about moving his backpack. I glanced around to make sure a seat was still open at the table behind us for Zach. Tables fill up fast. Most tables were full—only Shelly sat in a corner alone with her back to everyone else. I slid Zach's backpack into the open seat.

"What've you got today?" Brad asked around a mouthful of chicken nugget.

I tilted my thermos in his direction. "Mac and cheese."

"Oh, man. That is *not* mac and cheese. Mac and cheese is nuked for three minutes with cheese powder and milk. That is . . . I don't know what that is. But it's so much more than mac and cheese. Is that bacon on top?"

I nodded and laughed at Brad's groan. "Five cheeses, too. Mom bakes it."

Brad threw his half nugget onto the plastic tray. "Life is not fair."

He didn't mean anything by it, but suddenly both of us got quiet.

"What's going on with you, Caleb?" Brad finally said. "I mean, suddenly everything is so . . ."

"Nothing." I unwrapped a tub of thick chocolate pudding.

"Something happened," Brad said. "Does it have to do with recess? I already told Jett he's out. He's not going to play with us again, I'll make sure of it—"

"Why'd you do that?" I snapped. "He's a good player."

"I'd rather play with you," Brad said.

More awkward silence.

"Is it that kit you were writing about?"

I coughed on the pudding. "It's not a kit like something to make. Kit . . . Kit is a girl."

"*Oh*," Brad said slowly, his eyes suddenly widening and his face going shiny. "A *girl*." He laughed.

"Not like that!" When he laughed, I threw the cookie I had been unwrapping at his head. Brad caught it (of course) and popped it into his mouth. "Just a person . . . who happens to be a—"

"—*girl*," Brad drew out the word. "Where did you meet her?"

"She lives in the woods. Behind my house."

"Hmm. You should introduce us," Brad said. "Maybe she has a friend." He winked like a television bad guy and laughed. Believe it or not, we'd never talked about girls before. I mean, I had noticed, of course, that girls suddenly seemed to get blushy and giggly around Brad and, yeah, I noticed the girls themselves. But we didn't, like, talk about them.

"Shelly would be crushed." I laughed.

Brad threw a carrot stick at me. Of course I didn't catch it. The carrot just whapped me in the forehead.

-»»».«««-

Brad walked with me to my house after school. "So," he said, and stood on the tips of his toes to scan the woods. "Wanna introduce me to this girl? What's her name—Kate?"

"Kit," I corrected. "Nah, I've got that essay to write, remember? You do, too. Tomorrow's the last day of school!"

"Exactly." Brad grinned. "No way Mrs. Richards is going to grade it. It's a waste of time. I doubt she even reads them."

Brad tossed his backpack onto the porch. "Come on," he said, "let's go."

I stayed put, my hand on the door handle. "Yeah, but we have to read the essays in class. So even if she doesn't grade them, we've got to have *something* to hand in."

"Dude." Brad put his hands on my shoulders. "Relax. Tomorrow's Friday *and* the last day. No way is she going to bother grading them. Let's go."

"I don't—"

Brad groaned, throwing his hands up in the air now. "You don't *what*, man?"

I don't want you to steal her away from me. I don't want you to suck up all the oxygen around me. I don't want to be your sidekick—

But before I could push aside all of those truths and come up with a suitable lie for why I didn't want Brad to meet Kit, Mom saved me. "Caleb," she said as she opened the door, the cooler air-conditioned air sending chills across my flaming face, "sorry, but you don't have time to play outside today. I'm making an early dinner so Patrick has time to eat before track practice."

"Fine," I snapped. I don't know why I was mad at Mom suddenly, even though she had saved me from fighting with Brad. But I was.

"See you tomorrow," Brad said behind me. "Better get started on that *essay*."

I slammed the door and rushed to the window, checking to make sure Brad walked past the woods and back to the road. When he reached the edge of my yard, he whipped around and I ducked. When I sneaked back up to peek, he was heading toward his house.

"What was that about?" Mom asked. "Sounded like you and Brad were kind of fighting?"

I glanced at Mom. Her long red hair was pulled back in a ponytail. Her eyes, huge and watery brown like mine, followed Brad's retreating steps from the window. I shrugged. "Nothing."

"Sounded like something," she said.

"Is something burning?" I asked instead of answering.

"Shoot!" Mom scurried back into the kitchen, me trailing behind.

Two grilled steaks with salads were on plates. In the saucepan, a slightly thicker steak sizzled, an island in a melted butter ocean. Mom flipped the steak, sending flecks of hot butter popping into the air. She drizzled olive oil on top of the meat, and then spooned more of the butter on top of that.

"Looks great," Patrick said as he grabbed one of the plates already filled with a regular oil-free steak and the salad with nuts and some dressing. "Thanks, Mom." He sliced a piece of meat off the steak, wrapped the rest in aluminum foil, and put it in the fridge. "I'll eat the rest after practice."

Mom smiled and kissed his cheek. Then she slid the steak from the pan onto my plate, the fat, butter, and oil seeping from it onto the lettuce. My plate already had salad, topped with nuts and seeds, mounds of shredded cheese, and thick ranch dressing. "Here you go, sweetie," she said. Then she tipped my meds into my palm. I swallowed all eight pills with just one swig of water. She sighed but didn't give me the you're-going-to-choke lecture.

I nabbed the plate and sat beside Patrick. Mom raised an eyebrow when I cut off a chunk of squishy fat. "It's gross," I muttered.

Mom sighed but turned toward Patrick. "How was your day, love?"

"I heard back from Dr. Edwards," Patrick said. "He said he'll give me a recommendation for an internship." He grinned at Mom, and I swear the kitchen light made his white teeth glint. I forced a giant glob of steak down my throat while Mom made this high-pitched squealy sound she reserves for Patrick's accomplishments. I've heard it a lot.

"Wait, *my* Dr. Edwards?" I asked a second later.

"Yeah." Patrick didn't meet my eyes, just sliced off another small portion of steak and stabbed a piece of lettuce to go with it.

"Why would you need a letter of recommendation from *my* Dr. Edwards?"

Patrick didn't say anything. Mom brushed her hand across the top of mine. "Patrick is applying for a position at the Cystic Fibrosis Foundation, working on raising awareness and fund-raising this summer. Isn't that amazing?"

Suddenly I felt hot, like my skin—especially my face—had been dunked in simmering water.

"Why cystic fibrosis?" I managed. "Of all the foundations in the world, why the Cystic Fibrosis Foundation?"

Patrick's eyes narrowed. His nose flared a little while he breathed in and out, and he mashed his lips together like they were glued. He threw his crumpled napkin on the table. "Thank you for dinner, Mom. It was great." Patrick stood, making his chair rattle as it skid backward.

I stared at my buttery steak, at the way the brownish-red juices swirled into the melted butter but didn't mix with it, waiting for Mom to break apart the thick silence.

"I would've thought you'd be honored, Caleb," she half whispered. "Patrick has dozens of opportunities this summer. Coach Dan offered him a spot leading a summer running club for the middle school. He could've taught private violin lessons. Your father even secured a spot for him at his office. But instead of all of those, Patrick wants to raise awareness for cystic fibrosis." Mom reached over her plate to mine, cutting the steak into small pieces. I guess I wasn't eating fast enough. Finally, she said, "Why cystic fibrosis? You know why."

"Am I supposed to say thank you or something?" I snapped.

"That'd be nice." Mom laughed, but in a hard, not-at-all-funny way.

"You think he's doing it for me, but he isn't," I whispered.

"That's ridiculous. Who else would he be doing it for?" Mom said.

"Himself. So he can keep being the stupid hero," I muttered.

"What?" she asked.

I didn't answer. She took another heavy breath and threw her napkin on her plate, too. They were so alike; sometimes seeing it was like getting a paper cut across my chest. I glared at my plate, feeling my eyes sting and not able to put how I felt into words.

"Eat your steak." Mom opened her laptop and starting answering e-mails but I knew she was making sure I finished my food. I shoveled it into my mouth as fast as I could chew. Patrick swiped Mom's car keys from the counter to head to track practice and said bye to her but not me, not that I cared. I didn't even look up when he walked by smelling like deodorant. Finally, with only a few sprigs of lettuce and globs of dressing left on my plate, I asked if I could be excused.

"Yes, but I don't want you parking yourself in front of the TV," she said without looking up from her own screen.

"I—I thought I'd go for a walk," I said.

This time Mom did look up. "A walk?" she repeated like I had actually said I wanted to swap my fingers for hot dogs or something.

"Yeah, it's where you go outside and move your legs back and forth so they propel you forward."

Mom twisted her lips together but couldn't hold in a laugh. "Yes, I know what a walk is. If you hold up for a minute—let me finish this message—I'll join you. It's so nice out tonight!"

"That's okay," I said quickly. "I . . . I kind of want to be alone. You know, to think."

Mom smiled and she ruffled my hair. "That's a good idea. Take your phone with you, just in case."

⟴ ⟩⟩⟩ ⟨⟨⟨ ⟳

This time I didn't hesitate after entering the woods, just walked straight ahead.

When I reached the stream, I spotted Kit right away, sitting on the golden rock like a mermaid. "I was wondering if you'd show up tonight," she said.

"Here I am." I kept it cool—just smiling a little—but really I wanted to fist pump the air. I hadn't been sure she'd be there. Maybe part of me still thought she hadn't been real.

Kit patted the space on the rock next to her. "Room for two."

"My mom thinks I'm taking a walk." I kicked off my sneakers and skipped on rocks across the stream to Kit.

"Well, you walked here, didn't you?" Kit reached out her hand to help me up the rock. She was right; both of us fit.

"I thought you looked like a mermaid," I blurted.

Kit smiled as she kicked out her legs like a tail in front of her. "Then you're a sailor."

I sucked on my bottom lip, thinking about how Brad would bust a gut at what I was about to say and reminding myself that he didn't even know about this place. I glanced around, just to be sure. "Maybe my ship just crashed on the rocks?" I whispered, pushing the part of me that felt stupid for playing pretend into a little ball in my gut.

Kit nodded, her eyes getting rounder and brighter. "You need me to save you."

"And you need me to grow legs."

My cell phone buzzed in my pocket, breaking the spell. I fished it out and stared at the text from Mom. *R U OK?*

Kit read it over my shoulder and raised an eyebrow at me. I typed back. *Yes. Ran into a friend. OK?*

Immediately, Mom typed back. *Be back by dark. Tell Brad I said hi.*

I started to write back, but Kit put her hand over mine. With her other hand, she pointed to a tree beside the stream where two squirrels chittered. "Messengers from the sea witch have spotted us, Sailor Caleb! Let's hide in the forest!"

-》》》·《《《-

As soon as I could leave the house the next evening, I trailed through the woods to Mermaid Rock, where Kit was waiting. It had been the last day of school; Brad and a bunch of guys were going out for pizza to celebrate. But I told them I had other plans. "Writing another essay?" Brad had asked but let it go when Jett pointed out that everyone else would meet at the park to play football after eating.

Kit didn't ask anything about school. She didn't want to know how the last day was or how I had gotten away from Mom and Patrick this time (I told them I was meeting a friend—not mentioning that the friend wasn't Brad). Kit just launched right back into the story from the day before, where she was a recovering mermaid and I was an avenging sailor.

The sun slipped behind the trees, making lightning bug butts glow, when I told Kit good-bye.

"See you Monday morning?" she asked. "School's over, right?"

"I have to go to camp at the park. It's stupid, but I've got to go."

"Says who?" She raised her eyebrow.

"My mom," I answered automatically.

"Do you always do what your mom says?"

"Yeah." I snorted. "Most of the time."

"Maybe you should do what you want to do."

"It doesn't work that way." I pulled on my shoes and socks at the stream's edge. "Not for me."

When I looked up, Kit was gone.

I guess I wasn't as careful as I should've been as I headed home. When I opened the screen door, Patrick was sitting by the window. "Hanging out at Brad's, huh?" he asked, and I knew he had spotted me leaving the woods from the opposite direction of Brad's house. *Next time*, I told myself, *I'll find a different spot, one closer to the street.*

Mom saved me from replying by walking into the living room with my vest and a nebulizer treatment. "Hey! I was just about to call Brad's house to get you to come home." I shrugged and put the mask over my mouth and nose as Mom plugged in the nebulizer. Within seconds, the machine turned liquid medicine into a mist that I breathed in through the mask. Maybe this time the medicine would be serum. Maybe I'd wake up strong as a superhero, as magical as Kit.

CHAPTER THREE

"Do you have everything you need?" Mom asked for about the thirtieth time that Monday.

I nodded, but she grabbed my bag anyway and checked. "Caleb!" she scolded. "Your cell phone is only half charged! What if it dies during camp?"

"It won't," I said, staring out the car window. All around us, kids were running from their cars with beach blankets and water bottles, barreling ahead to the pavilion where camp counselors were checking them in. Some were already wearing swim trunks. None of them had parents with them.

"And you already have a layer of sunscreen on, right?" Mom asked.

"Yes!" I snapped. "You watched me put it on before we left, remember?"

Mom huffed. "I have a busy day today, Caleb. If you need any-thing, I'm not going to be able to leave the office, and it's Patrick's first day at his internship—"

"I get it," I grumbled. "I'll call Dad if I get sick or something."

Mom didn't say anything. She didn't have to. We both knew Dad wouldn't answer the phone.

"I still don't see why—"

This time Mom cut me off. "I'm not discussing this again, Caleb. You're not staying home by yourself."

"I'm twelve years old! I can handle it!"

"No." Mom opened the door to leave but just as abruptly slammed it shut and leaned into me. "Caleb, you need to get out and enjoy life, do fun things like camp, instead of sitting home alone. It's important."

I pointed to the port-a-potty in front of our car. "You think this is going to be fun?"

"Ugh!" Mom threw her arms in the air, slamming them down on the steering wheel. "Would you stop taking yourself so seriously? Just have fun? Just be a kid? For once, Caleb. Go and have fun, and let me go to work without feeling like the worst mom in the world!"

"So sorry to ruin your life!" I opened my door, hopped out of the car, and stomped toward the pavilion.

"Caleb, wait!" Mom was right on my heels. "I need to talk with the counselors."

"You already did, remember?"

"Yes, I talked with the organizer last night, but I have no idea if that person actually passed on the message to these guys."

"*Mom!* You're the only parent here . . ."

She stared straight ahead not looking at me.

I grabbed her arm, trying to hold her back. "*I* can tell them the rules," I hissed.

Mom shook off my grip, looking at me at last. She raised her other hand, shaking my backpack a little and then pushing it into my arms. "I can't even count on you to remember your backpack let alone to tell the counselors your restrictions. Besides, most of these kids have been going here for years. I need to at least introduce myself and you."

I glanced around. She was right. Kids were giving counselors fist bumps and laughing, already fitting in. I didn't see anyone I knew all that well. Our town was small enough that I knew most of the other kids' faces, but I didn't know *them*. This was my first summer having to do camp. Usually Mom took a couple weeks' vacation at the start of summer break, then Dad would do the same. But Dad had moved in with his girlfriend six months ago and said the cruise they went on together shortly afterward used up all his vacation. (And "besides, Caleb, you'd be bored out of your mind. What do Kristie and I know about entertaining a twelve-year-old?")

I used to hang out with Brad at his house for the rest of my summer break. We were friends for so long that Mrs. Williams—his

44

mom—knew everything there was to know about me. But this year, Brad had football practice every day. And with Patrick's internship, that left town camp as my only option.

And that meant I'd spend nine hours every day at the town park, being watched by counselors only two or three years older than me, hanging out on the baby playground or in the swimming pool with kids as young as five, all of us wearing matching electric-green T-shirts and being miserable. Well, I guess the last part wasn't a requirement, strictly speaking, but it was a given, for sure.

I trailed behind Mom as she made her way to the counselors. I recognized one from the bus, a girl named Ava with hair so long I doubted she had ever cut it. It hung in a blondish-brown braid down her back. She was one of those girls whose smile seemed to stretch to her ears but never her eyes, like she wanted you to smile back more than she really wanted to smile at you. Just picture the kid who always volunteers for every single position. That's Ava. *I should introduce her to Patrick,* I thought. No one out-volunteers Patrick. I smirked a little, thinking of how Ava and Patrick might duke it out to see who was the best all-around person.

Mom squeezed my shoulder. "That's a much better attitude," she said, I guess thinking my smirk was a this-might-not-be-so-bad-after-all smile. I rolled my eyes and she dropped her hand.

"You must be Caleb Winchester," Ava said in a super chipper voice as we approached. She put out her hand to shake.

"We ride the same bus," I said, shoving my fists into my pockets.

Mom grabbed Ava's hand. "I'm Stephanie. I need to go over a few of Caleb's restrictions."

"Let me guess," came a snarly voice behind me. "You're going to need the pavilion to be air-conditioned."

Sure enough, when I turned around there was Shelly Markel sitting on a picnic bench with her legs crossed at the ankles and looking as miserable as me in her electric-green T-shirt. Awesome. As if I weren't already dreading camp.

"*Mom*," I hissed. Mom's eyes darted from me to Shelly and back. For once in her life, she actually seemed to understand me. "Could we discuss these issues privately for a moment?" Mom asked Ava.

Ava's smile stretched farther (to the point of having to hurt and possibly being impossible). It was like she was trying to smile Mom into trusting her. Ava turned toward Shelly. "Shelly, sweetheart, why don't you go join the other campers?"

"I'm fine here." Shelly nibbled at a fingernail.

Ava's smile shook, but she kept the same too-bright voice as she said, "Shelly. Go. Now."

Shelly rolled her eyes. It took her the length of a mega sigh to reach her feet. As if she were part turtle, she ambled away.

"Now," Ava said, crossing her arms, "what would you like us to know? I'm sure you're aware that all counselors are CPR certified and graduated from the Red Cross babysitting class."

"Yes, I'm aware," Mom said, and glanced at her watch.

"Most parents are a little nervous about dropping off their children on the first day of camp. We'll keep a special eye on your little man. Don't worry, Mrs. Winchester."

I groaned and Ava's smile turned to a grimace for a half second.

Mom stiffened, her neck rising, her expression reading: I'm-about-to-offer-an-education. I've seen this face a lot. Oh, man. Here we go. "It's *Ms.* Baker, thank you," she said, each word sounding like a bite into a crisp apple. "And I have more concerns than the typical nervous mommy. My son has cystic fibrosis, which means he needs quite a bit more attention than simply being around someone who is CPR certified, although that is certainly lovely. Caleb's lungs are filled with thick, sticky mucus and easily become infected. He's going to cough a lot—and that's a good thing. The *not coughing* is when we need to be concerned. He also has to eat all of his lunch." Mom zipped open the backpack and pulled out my enormous lunch box. "Even if he doesn't want to, you need to make sure he eats it."

"Mom!" I grabbed the bag back from her, zipping it up. "I'm twelve years old. I can tell her what I need."

Ava's eyes widened when I told her my age.

"Yes," I said, "twelve."

"Wow," Ava murmured.

Mom continued on her tirade. "If he goes into distress, call me. If he seems tired, let him rest, but call me. If he needs to use the

47

facilities,"—Mom jerked her head toward the port-a-potty—"let him, without hesitation. If it's humid, let him sit in the shade, and call me." Mom said all of these quickly, as if I weren't standing right there.

"*Mom!*" I said again, noticing Shelly sneaking around the edge of the pavilion.

"*Ms. Baker*," said Ava, leaning in, the smile stretching to dangerous new levels, "I will learn absolutely everything there is to know about cystic fibrosis tonight and will be prepared to be in constant contact today. Do. Not. Worry."

Mom's head jerked back a millimeter. "Okay," she said. "I won't."

Mom leaned down to kiss the top of my head, but I ducked out of her way. "I have to keep you safe," she murmured.

"*I* can keep me safe," I snapped back.

Mom sighed but headed toward the car. I slumped onto a bench farthest from Shelly and put my head on my arms. Suddenly I heard Mom's voice, slightly out of breath. "One more thing," she said to Ava, "on days that I know will be too hot or too humid, or times when he just isn't feeling up to it, Caleb will need to stay home. Should I call you on those days?"

Ava shook her head. "Not necessary. I can mark him down as being one of our drop-in campers. That way, he can come when he's able but we won't necessarily count on him being here every day."

"*He* is right here," I said without lifting my head.

"That sounds great," Mom said over me.

About three hours later, I realized there's only so much you can do with sidewalk chalk.

Ava was determined we campers "cover the blacktop with color!" (Something she repeated about a thousand times.) I had dragged out snack time, slowly eating a couple cookies meant for lunch dessert in addition to the apple with peanut butter Mom had labeled *Snack*. (She's a little intense about how much I eat and when.) But soon there was nothing left to do but pick up a piece of chalk and hunker down on a bare patch of blacktop.

"Wanna help me draw a puppy?" a little kid asked, her knees covered in purple and yellow chalk.

"No," I said.

"How about a princess?"

"No."

"Why not?"

"Because I'm going into seventh grade and seventh graders don't draw princesses and puppies."

The girl's eyes got super wide. "You're in seventh grade?"

"Yes."

"Whoa! I'm in third. Everyone here is in third or fourth, 'cept for her." She pointed at Shelly. "What *do* seventh graders draw with chalk?"

I didn't answer, just wrote *My life sucks* on the pavement.

The girl scratched out *sucks* with pink chalk. "Mom says that's a swear. And you can't say swears."

"I wrote it. I didn't say it."

"You're not a nice seventh grader." The girl stood, crossed her arms, and stomped away to sit next to an apparently nicer kid who was drawing a yellow duck. I turned away from them and drew cube after cube after cube.

"That's creative," Shelly snarked.

I glanced at what she was drawing. It was a series of complicated hexagons interlacing. "What's that supposed to be?" I asked because I was bored, and *not* because I cared what Shelly was up to.

"A mandala," she said in an isn't-it-obvious way. "It symbolizes the universe."

"Whatever," I muttered and drew another cube. "So, how did you end up getting stuck here?"

Shelly broke her chalk pressing it into the blacktop. "Ava is my cousin."

As I drew, I kept glancing up at the port-a-potty. Every time the door opened or closed, the squeaky bang made everyone look. No way would anyone be able to head in there undetected.

"Why don't you just go already?" said Shelly, following my gaze. "Or are you afraid you're going to fall in?"

But at that moment, Ava clapped her hands and finally said what

50

I had been both waiting for and dreading all morning. "All right, campers! Time for the pool!" I'd been waiting for this because swimming is awesome. I'd also been dreading it because the pool is open to the public, which meant anyone who was there would see right away that I was at day camp like a baby. *At least there's actual plumbing— and flushing toilets—in the pool house*, I told myself.

We grabbed towels from our bags and headed toward the pool in a line behind Ava. "Okay, guys," she said, and held up her hand for us to be quiet. "We've got two hours to swim before lunch. Have fun, and remember to listen to the lifeguards!"

"You're not going in?" Shelly asked.

Ava shook her head. "Nope, the lifeguards take over watching you guys during pool time. But, listen,"—she leaned in toward Shelly. I paused, too, to eavesdrop—"I promised your mom I'd keep an eye on you. Make sure you made an effort to make friends."

Shelly stomped away. I waited a few seconds before heading into the pool area, figuring all the kids would run straight ahead into the water. I was right; all of them were already splashing around, with the exception of Shelly, who sat on a lounge chair. She slipped a book out from the middle of her folded towel and buried her nose in it.

When I figured the changing room would be empty, I gave in to the cramping in my gut and ducked into the men's side. But I was out of luck. Even though all of the other campers were in the water, the changing room was packed with people. A dad was squishing his toddler into a swim diaper. An old man was at the mirrors, adjusting a black swim cap over his wrinkly head. Another kid snapped on goggles and smeared on some sunscreen. Worse of all, a bathroom attendant stood in the corner, playing on an app on his phone.

But it was this or the port-a-potty. Not making eye contact with anyone, I went straight to the toilet and locked the door behind me. It was one of those public bathroom stalls where the door has a half-inch gap so I could still see out. I bit my lip and tried to wait until just about everyone trickled out, then did my business.

The truth is, cystic fibrosis is more than muck-filled lungs and lots of infections, though I was thankful Mom didn't go into too many bathroom details in her crash course for Ava. The worst part about being a twelve-year-old kid with mild cystic fibrosis, if you ask me, is the poop.

People with CF can have some issues with Number Two, if you know what I mean. Because my body sucks at absorbing the nutrients it needs—especially fat and protein—I have to eat a lot of food. And because my pancreas is whacked-out, getting rid of all that food is an issue. I either have trouble going or I go all the time. All. The. Time.

And, okay, here's another thing about CF: Not only is the poop a problem, the poop itself is . . . well, extra gross. I mean, even more than regular poop. Let's just say Mom lights a lot of candles and we have lots of air filters stationed outside the bathroom at home.

Being stressed out all morning about using the bathroom was

making everything—and I mean, everything—worse. I prayed for a silent, quick go. No luck. My lower stomach cramped and rumbled, as if laughing out loud at my prayers.

I pressed my lips together to keep from whimpering and just gave up on holding back.

The attendant coughed. He gagged. "You okay, man?" he asked a minute later.

"I'm fine," I managed.

"I can call someone if you want. You one of the campers?"

"No! No, I'm fine!"

"Don't sound—don't smell—fine," he muttered. A few seconds later, I heard this high-pitched whizzing sound. I peeked through the gap in the door. The attendant was spraying air freshener directly at my stall.

"Come on, man!" I grimaced. My face was sweaty and all I could think of was finishing this and cooling off in the water.

"You almost done?" the attendant asked.

I flushed the toilet harder than necessary, swung open the door, and stomped to the sink to wash my hands.

"If you've got the squirts, you're not allowed to swim. Pool rule," Attendant Guy said.

"I don't have diarrhea. That's just how my . . . that's just how I go, okay?"

"Did an animal die inside you, kid?"

"You know what—"

But whatever I was about to yell at this guy—and I didn't really know what would've come out of my mouth, only that it'd be as ugly as what just happened in that stall—was cut short by a rush of guys coming into the bathroom. Great. The football team. This was the first year our town had a football team, so practice began right at the end of the school year. Which meant the team went straight to the pool after practice. Which meant I'd see them all every horrible day of camp.

"Oh, puke!" gagged the first one, Jett. "What the heck happened in here?"

The attendant didn't say anything, just sprayed more freshener. My own nose crinkled at the new stench—sweat and dirt—as the rest of the guys followed behind Jett. All of them gagged or coughed or covered their noses as they rushed in.

"Ugh! Fried farts and onion!" boomed someone still in the hall, but of course I knew who it was before he entered.

"Hey, Brad," I muttered, praying the attendant wouldn't rat me out. Brad was all too familiar with my digestive issues from all the times I spent in the bathroom at his house, so I knew he'd cover for me if anyone pointed a finger in my direction. "Yeah, some old man was just in here. Must've had sauerkraut for breakfast or something."

The attendant coughed, but Brad ignored him.

"Caleb! Sweet! I didn't know you'd be here!"

"Yeah, Mom dropped me off this morning." I didn't mention that it was because of camp, although Brad's eyes dropped to my T-shirt.

"Cool," he said, and turned toward his team. "Last one in the water is a loser!"

"Hey!" the attendant yelled over the insults being slung back and forth among the team. "You've got to shower before getting in the water when you're dirty and sweaty. Pool rule!"

But Brad—and then everyone else—ignored him, rushing out to the water. I trailed behind them. "Jerks," I heard the attendant mutter as he doused the room with more air freshener spray.

⇒﹥﹥﹥.⫷⫷⫷⟵

"What are you doing here?" Shelly snapped a half hour later when I crashed on the lounge chair next to hers. "Shouldn't you be out there, with them?"

"I don't want to swim anymore." My wet T-shirt stuck to my chest and weighed about a million pounds.

"You know you're supposed to take your shirt *off* to swim, right?" Shelly wiped at the drops of water I accidentally flicked onto her when wringing out the corner of my shirt.

"I didn't feel like it," I said. More like I didn't feel like having her point out that she could count my ribs or notice how scrawny my arms are, not that Shelly needed to know any of that. I shook out the shirt, splattering her.

55

"Overcome with camp pride?"

I turned on my side, away from her. "I didn't want to take off my shirt, okay? Get over it. At least I don't come to the pool to read."

Shelly turned the page of her book with a snap.

"Come on, Caleb! We need another for volleyball!" Brad shouted from the pool.

"Nah, you guys go ahead," I said.

"Awesome," Jett called out. "Then we can get started." He spiked a beach ball at Brad, who, of course, popped it over Jett's head, scoring a point.

→≫≫‹‹‹←

"You smell like chlorine." Mom buried her nose in my hair as we sat at a red light. She had picked me up from camp to go straight to a checkup.

"I don't think Dr. Edwards cares what my hair smells like."

"So, camp," Mom said. "Not so bad, right?"

I didn't answer, just turned away from her. I wasn't about to tell her how Jett snickered when our pool time was over and Ava made us line up by age to check us in. "Look," he had said loud enough for me to hear, "Caleb's shorter than the fourth grader in front of him." I didn't tell her how Brad didn't say anything, only dunked Jett and swam like a fish to the other side of the pool. I didn't tell her how the bathroom attendant groaned when I walked to the stall during after-lunch pool time or about how all day long I only thought about Kit. Do homeschooled kids get the summer off, too? What was she doing all day? Would she be on Mermaid Rock after dinner tonight, hoping I'd join her?

I followed Mom into the doctor's office. We each grabbed one of the paper masks by the door and slid them over our faces. I used to love pretending like I was a doctor instead of a patient when I was younger and did this. Now it just felt routine. Mom went to check me in and I followed a nurse straight into an exam room off the lobby. It's dangerous for CF patients to breathe in the same air, since we can transfer dangerous viruses and bacteria to one another pretty easily, so Dr. Edwards makes sure patients are separated from the moment we walk into the office. The door was open, though, so I could see and hear Mom.

Just then, a couple walked in with a baby. The nurse led them into a room on the other side of the lobby from me, but I could hear the baby wailing. Soon the baby's mom waited behind my mom. Even though the baby was in the room with the dad, the woman rocked back and forth as if she were holding the baby. I couldn't look away from her for some reason. The woman's face was pale and her eyes huge and unblinking.

"First visit?" Mom asked her. The woman nodded. *Portrait of a Mother in Shock.*

Mom's eyes got watery. She did this thing when we were at

doctor appointments and she saw new parents like this. I doubt she even knew she did it. She talked too loud, was too chipper, and, in my opinion, way too obvious.

"We've been seeing Dr. Edwards for years. Had to leave summer camp today for the appointment," she said. "My son's twelve. He swam all day, I bet."

The mom didn't say anything, just tilted her head toward the room on the other side where the baby was still crying.

Mom continued anyway. "Some of his friends on the football team were there. He has so many friends!"

I rolled my eyes. The nurse behind the desk motioned Mom forward. "Just here for a routine check," Mom said, again too loudly and too obviously for the woman's benefit instead of the nurse's. "I can't wait to hear what Dr. Edwards has to say. I bet Caleb's grown two inches since last year!"

The nurse clacked on the keyboard in front of her. "I see that Caleb was treated for a lung infection two months ago. Any lingering issues?"

"No," Mom said, her voice too bright. "Rebounded so well! He's just a *totally typical* twelve-year-old boy!"

"Go on back," the nurse said.

"Good luck! I'm sure you're going to be just fine," Mom said to the woman before leaving the line.

"What?" the woman said, finally blinking.

The woman hadn't been listening at all.

Sometimes Mom was so dumb. That family wouldn't have noticed if Captain America himself stood in front of them, telling them, "It's not the end of the world." They had just found out their kid had cystic fibrosis. Their minds were probably stuck on phrases like *stunted growth* and *frequent hospitalizations* and, most especially, *shortened lifespan*. I remember the gut punch I felt the first time I googled CF and read: *Patients who live until adulthood have a median predicted survival age of forty.*

When we left an hour later, I still heard crying from the baby's room. But it wasn't from the baby.

By the way, I had barely grown half an inch.

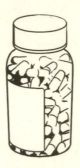

CHAPTER FOUR

I was a tree, stretching toward the sun overhead. I shook out my limbs, twisting so my leaves warmed in the light, sending a shudder down my trunk. But the trembling didn't matter—I wasn't worried—because I somehow felt my roots digging deeper and much, much wider under the earth. Those roots grasped the dirt and held tight so those upper branches could soak up the sunlight like a kid drinking forbidden soda through a straw.

"Wake up, sleepyhead." Mom's cool hand across my cheek pulled me from the dream. "You fell asleep during your treatment again."

It took me a second to remember where I was. The sun wasn't up yet, so for a moment I thought it was the middle of the night. Plus, I still felt the shaking through my trunk—I mean, my body. Mom unclasped the clips of my vest as I removed the nebulizer mask from my face.

Every morning, I woke up at 4:45 a.m., strapped on the vest that shook and beat against my ribs, and secured the nebulizer mask over my face. I usually watched a superhero movie while sitting there, but almost every morning, I fell back asleep. Sounds crazy, doesn't it? Falling asleep while breathing in medicine and having something beat on your body. But I got used to it, I guess. Sort of like how I got used to missing the read-aloud story before lunch every day, since I had to go to the nurse for percussions. (Basically, that means she beat on my back with a little handheld bowl-like thing to get the mucus moving. I think she kind of looked forward to it.)

I huffed and coughed, bringing up thick gunk that had been trapped in my lungs. A lot of people think cystic fibrosis is a lung issue. It's really not. It's a cellular problem. Because of a messed-up gene, my body doesn't make regular thin mucus to protect my lungs or regular sweat to clean out my body or enzymes that digest food. Those juices are supposed to be kind of watery, made to make everything nice and slippery so nutrients and oxygen can flow though my body and the bad stuff gets a quick exit. Only my juices aren't slippery at all. They're more like pulpy orange juice. That's not quite right. Think thick, sticky goo. And instead of making it easier for everything to pass, that goo is like a clog, making it harder for the stuff I need— nutrients and oxygen—to get through my body and the stuff I need to lose—bacteria and viruses—to leave. Maybe someday doctors will figure a way to fix that whacked-out gene and my body will stop being a mucus factory. Until then, I have to take my meds and wear this vest. All that rumbling helps break up the mucus. The nebulizer medicine I breathe in makes my lungs open up a little. Then I cough out the gunk. The whole thing, I realize, is kind of gross.

I barely stopped coughing when Mom pushed meds and a glass of water toward me. I took two different antibiotics morning and night, every single day, whether I had a virus or bacteria or not. Next up, vitamins, since my body only absorbed about half to a quarter of what it was supposed to take in from the food I ate. Then some acid reflux medication since that whole not digesting thing, as previously discussed, wasn't exactly comfortable. Finally, Mom handed me one more pill.

"Are you serious?" I asked, eyeing the enormous yellow tablet. It had to be an inch long. "Are you sure you got the pill for scrawny twelve-year-olds and not big-butt rhinos?"

Mom crossed her arms. "You heard what Dr. Edwards said yesterday. It's an absolute miracle that you haven't been hospitalized more than you have—a lot of CF kids are admitted for two weeks every three months, routinely, just to stay strong. You're lucky all you have to do is down a rhino pill."

The liver pill was new—something Dr. Edwards added to my "regiment," as he called it, the day before. It's supposed to help bile work better. I didn't pay a lot of attention after Dr. Edwards said I didn't have to worry about it. I swallowed the pill, feeling it go sideways in my throat. I downed half the glass of water until the pill scratched its way to my gut. I choked down all the words I wanted to scream at Mom, too. *Lucky?* Was she serious?

"Do you need ten minutes?" she asked quietly, staring hard at my face.

I knew what she was asking. Whenever I whined about CF—like when I treaded water in the swim team's Guppy division while Brad and everyone else my age moved to Dolphin—Mom gave me ten minutes. Set a timer and everything. Ten minutes to feel sorry for myself, to complain and cry and let my mind sink to dark places. When the timer went off, I had to stop, even if I was still crying, and, as she put it, "move onward and upward."

I shook my head. "I'm good. Maybe I'll get so good at swallowing all these meds I can start a competitive eating club," I joked. "Move on to hot dogs or something."

Mom grinned and rubbed my head. As annoying as it was to have her constantly nagging and prodding, it was worse to see her sad for me. "Get dressed, and head down for breakfast. I'm dropping you off early at camp. I need to open the office this morning."

And just like that, I was back to being annoyed. I plopped onto the bed, wishing I actually was a tree. No one forced trees to go to summer camp with babies. "Mom! It's *summer*. Can't I sleep a little more? I'll walk to the park after breakfast!"

To my shock, she paused, thinking. Then her face set, her lips pressing together until they were white. "Not today. I need to talk to you about something and I only have time in the car."

"Oookay," I drawled, trying to figure out what was going on. I flipped through the appointment yesterday in my mind—did Dr. Edwards give her information he didn't give me? Were my numbers lower than they should be? I thought he seemed happy my lung function was about the same as a few months before. I pulled on another electric-colored camp T-shirt (blue, this time) and shorts, thinking hard. No, there wasn't a moment Mom wasn't with me. He couldn't have told her anything serious. So this wasn't about me or CF. What was it? It couldn't be anything about Patrick; he never caused her white-lip face. The only things that did were bad news about my CF and ...

"Your father ... ," Mom started, almost as soon as I buckled my seat belt a few minutes later.

"Is a total butthead," I finished.

Mom's mouth twitched for just a second. "That is *not* what I was going to say."

"But it *is* what you were thinking."

Mom turned her face to the street, but I could tell she was fighting a smile. "Are you going to add mind reading to your competitive eating plans?"

"Maybe." I laughed. "What is it, Mom? What did he do now?"

Dad left us about two years earlier. It wasn't a big deal. Life without him hadn't changed much except for the whole when's-Dad-coming-home question didn't have to be asked at every single dinner. Dad had checked out years ago, to be honest. He used to come home, all jazzed with new CF research he had found or he'd be spouting off what was working for someone he had met on a CF message board. But he hadn't done that for years. And before he left, there were lots of times when he didn't even come home. He worked in insurance, and that, for some reason, meant crazy long nights. At least, that's what I thought until I spotted a suitcase in the trunk one morning. He didn't come home that night or the next. The divorce was finalized a year ago. He lives with his girlfriend, Kristie, in a condo somewhere in Central Asia. Actually, it's about two miles from our house, but it was the same difference.

Aside from a few super awkward dinners each month—where Patrick droned on and on about his incredible accomplishments, and Kristie prattled on and on about how amazing Dad was, and Dad and I actively ignored each other—we never saw him. Which was fine by me.

I stared out the window as Mom drove down our street. The woods swallowed the early morning sunlight pouring over them. Man, I wished I were there. Kit's words echoed in my mind: *I do what I want.* "What do I have to do?" I asked Mom when the silence between us stretched longer than the woods.

She took a deep breath and continued like I had never interrupted her. "Your father will pick you up at three o'clock."

I made a puffing sound out of my nose.

"He'll be here, Caleb. He promised." We didn't speak again until she pulled into a parking spot at the park. Ava waved frantically from a picnic table and immediately jumped to her feet, striding toward us. Mom swore under her breath. To me, she said, "I have a stressful project at work. It's going to be a late night. Dad's either going to take you home, where Patrick will make you dinner, or he'll take you back to his place with Kristie." She always said Kristie's name with too much emphasis, like she was a cheerleader or something. It was her CF's-not-so-bad voice, and this time, I was the new parent.

"Whatever," I muttered.

Ava was now beside our door, tapping on Mom's window. "Ms. Baker!" she shouted through the glass. "Don't forget Caleb's Creon pills! I've packed candy bars if he needs extra caloric intake today! I spent all night studying and I know *everything* there is to know about CF now!" She grinned, her smile stretching so far the tendons in her neck popped.

"Can I have my ten minutes now?"

Mom's shoulders peaked and fell with a quick laugh. She gave Ava a thumbs-up and then turned back to me. "I'll see you tonight, Caleb. I'll call at eight—and I expect you to be doing your treatment by then."

"You're going to be that late?" I asked. Mom was a dental hygienist. The office closed at six. What kind of projects did dental hygienists have to do that late? "What about my meds and my treatment?"

"I wrote everything down. It's on the kitchen counter. Your meds are divvied out and ready to go, and the nebulizer's loaded." She ruffled my hair. "You'll be fine."

I stared into her eyes, seeing something there I didn't like. Makeup. And secrets. "A project, huh?"

"Mmhmm," Mom said as she rooted through my backpack, making sure I had tablets, snacks, lunch, and a fully charged phone.

And just like that, I knew. My mom was going on a date. "Will you be having lots of projects in the future?" I asked.

Mom smiled and bit her lip. "I hope so," she said quietly.

Ava tapped on the window again. "Don't forget sunscreen!" she chirped. "Antibiotics often cause sun sensitivity!"

"Bye, sweetheart." Mom lightly kissed my forehead. Her mouth was sticky. Lip gloss. "Remember, Dad will pick you up at three."

I grabbed my backpack from her lap and hoisted it onto my shoulder as I got out of the car. "Have a fun time on your . . . project."

Mom's cheeks were pink, but not from makeup. "Thanks, Caleb."

⇢⋙⋘⇠

Ava trailed me to the pavilion. "You're the first one here, aside from Shelly," she said. Her nose crinkled a little when she said her cousin's name. "This is perfect since I wanted to tell you a few things." I tucked my bag under the picnic table and put my head on my arms,

67

taking a cue from Shelly, who was doing the same thing at a corner table. She even snored a little. Drool trailed across her arm.

"What time did you guys get here?" I asked.

Ava shrugged. "I have to be here to set up and cover the earliest possible drop-off at six. So we get here about five thirty."

"Wow," I said under my breath. And I thought falling asleep with my vest was bad.

"So," Ava said, "I learned as much as I could last night about cystic fibrosis. Do you need a vest treatment midday?"

I felt my eyes turn wide as marbles. "No. At school, the nurse would sometimes do percussions but if we do something active—like swimming or the obstacle course—I should be all right." Usually in the summer, I'd jump on the trampoline in Brad's backyard after lunch to get my lungs working.

"Okay." Ava blinked, as if crossing off something on a mental to-do list. "Let me know if there is anything you need at all—extra rest, an alteration to the obstacle courses, high-caloric snacks, whatever you need." She patted my arm, looking a lot like a robot. I had a feeling she read one too many online how-to-talk-to-CF-kids articles. "I realize that the high physical and emotional impact of your diagnosis must weigh on you. I am here for you whenever you'd like to talk, whatever you'd like to discuss." All of this was said deliberately, clearly rehearsed.

Ava's scary-big grin pulled back farther. "Anything, Caleb.

Whatever you'd like to discuss. I've also researched many religions and cross-sectioned their beliefs."

I stared at her, momentarily confused. "You, like, want me to talk to you about Heaven and stuff?"

"If that's what you're comfortable discussing."

I wasn't. I wasn't comfortable talking with her about anything at all. "So you researched a lot about CF and now you're, like, an expert?"

"Right." Ava nodded. "I'm a really great researcher. Always have been. Don't feel at all like you're on your own." She awkwardly patted my hand again. "You're not. I understand."

"Oh, really?" I half laughed to myself. Kit's face popped into my head. That's not really right—her words did. *Maybe you should do what you want.* And in that moment, I wanted to make Ava realize she didn't understand squat of what it's like to be me. I looked her straight in her eager little eyes. "I read all about witches," I said. "So don't worry." Her smile wobbled. "I understand, too." This time I patted her hand.

Ava's mouth popped open. I was flooded with guilt. Did I really just say that? And, as if someone pulled the plug, I just as suddenly didn't care one bit. *Maybe you should do what you want.* Ava pulled back from the picnic bench, and I lowered my head onto my arms, pretending to fall asleep like Shelly.

"Anger is common. Bitterness and . . . meanness . . . it's normal." I knew, just knew, that once again she wore that hideously big smile.

Whatever. I felt Ava's stare on the top of my head but quickly fell into rhythm with Shelly's breath. Soon Ava sighed heavily and moved on to prep for more campers.

And I almost did fall asleep, but a low whistle made me pop my head up. In the corner of the pavilion, Shelly tilted her head up in my direction. "Wow, that was cold." She shuddered. "Didn't think you had that in you, Winchester."

I covered my head again.

⟶≫≫≪≪⟵

Remember how I felt like someone pulled a plug on that guilt? Well, it clogged right back up a few minutes later. I couldn't stop seeing Ava's hurt expression. The guilt building up in my chest forced me to be nice to Ava the rest of the day. I laughed at her stupid jokes ("You guys are starting to sizzle like bacon out there! Time for sunscreen!"), but there was no mistaking the strain behind her returned smiles. Even worse, they were mixed with pity.

"Caleb," she said after telling the campers it was snack time. I was pulling a package of Mom's granola and a container of thick yogurt from my lunch bag. My bottle of pills was next to my spoon. Ava leaned down so her mouth was close to my ear and she lowered her voice. "We have a staff bathroom on the side of the pool house. No one uses it except for me and Dave." She pointed to the other camp counselor, who was squirting antibacterial gel on campers' sticky

70

hands. "If you'd like a more private bathroom, I'll leave the key by my bag in the pavilion." She walked away before I could thank her.

Looked like Ava really was an incredible researcher. It was a little embarrassing, but not as much as having to face that bathroom attendant again.

→⟩⟩⟩⟩⟨⟨⟨⟨←

Here's a huge shocker to no one: three o'clock came and went and Dad never showed.

"Can we *go* yet?" Shelly whined to Ava as she plunked down a few feet from me at the parking lot's edge.

"Just as soon as Caleb is picked up," Ava said in a too-sweet voice. She checked her watch. To me, she added, "Want me to call him?"

I held up my cell phone. "I already did, three times. He hasn't picked up or answered my texts." The texts didn't even show *read,* meaning he was totally shutting me out. Like I said, shocker.

Shelly sighed and flung herself backward on the lawn. "Don't you live a half mile from here? Can't you just walk home so we can leave?"

"Shelly!" Ava gasped. "Caleb, I'm sure your dad's just running a little behind."

A half hour so far. Mom never would be this late. I thought about calling her, but then I remembered the lip gloss and her "project." I punched out a text to Patrick instead. *Dad hasn't picked me up yet. Have you heard from him? Supposed to be here at 3.*

Almost immediately, my phone rang. "I'm on my way," my brother said. His voice was gruff. He hung up before I could say thank you.

"You can go," I said to Ava. "Patrick's on his way. Should be here in, like, five minutes. You don't have to wait for me."

"Oh!" Ava's cheeks pinked a little. "Patrick?"

"Yeah," I said, "my brother."

"Oh!" she said again. Shelly groaned next to her. Ava smoothed her ponytail with her palms. That smile of hers suddenly didn't look forced. I smothered my own groan. It gets kind of old to constantly have girls fawning all over a person you know to be extremely boring and annoying. I mean, I guess Patrick is handsome in a brooding, always-right sort of way. He's got brown hair like me, but his is thicker and swoops over his forehead instead of just flopping to the sides. He also has greenish-brown (Mom calls them hazel) eyes, but they're tough to see behind the dark, thick eyebrows he's constantly scrunching together whenever he looks my way, like he's trying to solve a puzzle. Like I said, annoying.

"There he is!" Ava pointed down the sidewalk a minute or two later. Sure enough, there was my brother—as tall and strong as I was short and scrawny—striding purposefully toward us, clearly fuming. I guess I had interrupted violin practice, or maybe track, or chess, or some other amazing talent of his. "He's just like Heathcliff over the moors," Ava gushed.

"What?" Shelly and I said in unison, both of us whipping toward Ava, whose face was outright on fire now.

"Nothing! Nothing! I didn't say anything."

"Yes, you did," Shelly said. She crossed her arms.

"I said, 'It looks like we can go to the doors.' You know, the car doors. Like we can go to our car now that Patrick is here. Let's go." She threw her giant duffel bag full of camp supplies onto her shoulder and hoisted up a big box of sunscreen, sidewalk chalk, and bubbles.

"Hey, let me help." Patrick rushed forward, pulling the box from her arms. I swear, I thought Ava would faint. Under his breath, Patrick added, "Geez, Caleb. Think you could've noticed she needed help?"

"She just stood up! Just now! How was I supposed to—" But I stopped trying to defend myself, cut off by shock as a white convertible with Dad behind the wheel squealed into the parking lot.

Patrick followed my gaze. He huffed out of his nose. In the same gruff voice, he muttered, "Could he be any more of a cliché?"

Dad's face—a looser, tanner version of Patrick's—split into a grin. "I come for one son and see two!" He patted the side of the car with his hand, not bothering to get out. "What do you think?" he asked.

"I think you're forty minutes late," I said.

Dad waved his hand like my words were gnats. "Nah, I mean the car! Sweet, isn't it?"

"Mom's a payment behind on the station wagon," Patrick muttered a little louder.

At least Dad had the decency to flush a little. "This is Kristie's car. She's letting me borrow it today."

"Why? Is she out of town?" I asked hopefully.

"No, she's waiting for us at home." Dad's face was now familiar again, locked into a stony why'd-I-ever-have-kids glare. "She's making dinner." He shifted the car into park. "I wasn't expecting to see you here, Patrick. I'll tell her to make another plate for you."

Patrick quickly shook his head. "No, I came to bail you out, again. Caleb called when you didn't show."

"I'm a couple minutes late!" Dad growled. To me, he said, "If you're in such a hurry, why are you just sitting there. Get in!"

Patrick made a weird grabbing gesture toward me with the arm not holding the box of camp supplies. It was like he was going to pull me to him or something. Quickly, he dropped his arm. To Dad, he said, "I can take Caleb home with me. I'm already here."

The truth was, I totally would've rather gone back to our house. But I knew Mom would freak if she found out Dad had ditched me again. And there was that whole not-wanting-Patrick-to-be-the-hero thing, too. "That's okay," I said. I moved around to the other side of the car, waiting for Dad to unlock the door.

"Patrick, you're already here. Why don't you come back with us?" Dad asked. "Please?"

I sighed and moved into the cramped backseat, my knees up to my chin, feeling like a giant for the first time in my life.

CHAPTER FIVE

Kristie hugged me when I walked in the front door. She was about as opposite of Mom as a person could get. Her hair lay in a long dark braid to her waist. Her tall body was lean and muscly; I rarely saw her wearing anything but workout clothes. But the nice kind—you know, that a lot of moms have on all day long—not the ratty sweats and old T-shirts that Mom wore those few times she hopped on the elliptical at night. Not that Mom was fat or anything. She was pretty skinny; she was just soft. A hug from Mom was like being tucked in under a quilt at night. A hug from Kristie was like cuddling concrete.

"How are you, Caleb?"

"Fine," I said. I liked Kristie. She seemed nice and all. I just didn't like knowing her, if that made sense. I sometimes thought the feeling was mutual.

Kristie dropped her arms and gestured toward the kitchen. "We'll eat in about ten minutes if you'd like to wash up."

"It's only four thirty," I pointed out.

"Kristie likes to have all of her meals by five," Dad said from the doorway.

"It's important for digestion," she added brightly, patting her rock-hard, flat stomach.

Patrick trailed behind Dad. "Oh, Patrick!" Kristie exclaimed. "What a wonderful surprise!"

"Knew you wouldn't mind, darling," Dad said, and kissed Kristie's cheek while I tried not to puke into my mouth. "Should I throw another chicken breast on the grill?"

"No, that won't be necessary. I made extra for lunches tomorrow, so we'll have plenty."

"You think of everything. What I love about you." As the smooch-fest started anew, I escaped into the kitchen. I dumped my backpack next to the sink and rooted around for my evening meds. I swallowed all the other pills in one gulp but put the Creon bottle next to my place setting. How many Creon I took depended on the meal—heavy meals meant more tablets. Most dinners required about six to eight tablets.

Kristie quickly put out another placemat and dishes for Patrick as we sat down. Kristie brought out a giant bowl of salad, and Dad placed a platter of grilled chicken in the middle of the table. I chewed my lip, looking from the salad—one of those fancy ones with lots of lettuce that look like weeds—to the lean meat. "Shall we?" Dad said when no one moved.

"This is it?" I asked.

"Caleb!" Dad snapped. Kristie's smile wobbled.

"I didn't mean—"

"Could you be any ruder?" Dad crossed his arms. "Kristie worked hard on this meal. Be grateful!"

"It's just . . ."

Patrick cleared his throat. "Maybe if you have some salad dressing—ranch or blue cheese . . ."

Kristie, with two bright red spots on her cheeks, pushed forward a bowl of sliced lemons. "Your father and I usually squeeze lemon juice over our food."

"It's delicious," Dad said, and patted Kristie's hand. "Since I've moved in here, I've lost fifteen pounds."

"Imagine how much I'd lose," I muttered.

"Caleb." Dad groaned. "I'll take you out for ice cream on the way home, okay?"

Patrick stood. "Or do you have butter or peanut butter? Maybe Caleb could have a sandwich, too?"

Dad pulled on Patrick's arm. "Let's not hijack Kristie's dinner. She's sticking to a strict diet and cleaned out our pantry to stay true to it. We don't have sugar or fats in the house." Dad took a bite of chicken. "Like I said, I'll take you boys out for ice cream later. No big deal."

I shook out two tablets and helped myself to some chicken.

"It's incredible being engaged to a nutritionist," Dad said, his voice all casual and bright again. "I've learned so much about proper food consumption."

"You're a nutritionist?" Patrick asked. "I've been taking lessons from a nutritionist who works with Dr. Edwards, Caleb's doc."

I worked on not rolling my eyes.

Kristie patted her cheeks like she was cooling them off. "Well, I'm not technically a nutritionist, I suppose. Not licensed or anything. But nutrition consultant is what they're calling all the Poolside Body Works providers now." Kristie sells workout DVDs, supplements, and diet plans. It's why she's always in workout clothes, I guess, and why the convertible license plate is PULSID GRL.

Patrick cut into his chicken. "It's just most nutritionists study cystic fibrosis, from what I understand. Nutritionists know how important it is for people with cystic fibrosis to have a high-fat diet, that just to avoid starvation they need to eat twice the amount of food as the rest of us. And with Caleb spending the days at camp, being active, plus needing to actually grow, his demands are—"

"That's enough," Dad quietly warned.

"I didn't realize . . . ," Kristie mumbled. "I mean, this is a *healthy* meal."

I grunted but didn't say anything.

"Enough!" Dad said again. Now his face was red, too. "This is my home. This is my fiancée. This is what we have for dinner. Enough."

Patrick's eyes slid to mine and back to his plate. *She didn't realize?* She was marrying my dad and she never thought to even google cystic fibrosis? And Dad, he never thought to mention it or at least offer a *Hey, put some shredded cheese on the table tonight?*

"Eat," Dad said to us. "Just eat, and let's move on."

I forced my hands out from where I sat on them and cut into the chicken. It's not like I was hungry, anyway.

"Excuse me," Patrick said quietly. He pushed back his seat and went to his own backpack. He unzipped it and pulled out a can, but instead of soda it was a nutrient milkshake. He put it beside my plate. "Dr. Edwards had a bunch of these samples in the office today. He wanted me to bring one home for you."

I checked the can—high in fat and calories, plus chocolate flavored. "Thanks," I said. But honestly? I was kind of annoyed. Patrick, saving the day again.

I guess Dad was feeling the same way because now I could hear *his* teeth grinding as I popped the tab.

"If you like shakes, Caleb," Kristie said, "Poolside Body Works is starting a new body shake campaign in the fall. It works in two ways—a machine that literally shakes the fat right off your body in the form of a compression vest, plus low-cal, nutrient-dense shakes!

How convenient, right?" Kristie smiled as she talked, carefully scooping up shreds of lettuce.

"Yeah, super convenient," I said, thinking about how my vest was oh-so-convenient. "I know I *love* mine."

Dad ignored me, but Kristie said, "Oh, you have a vest? Is it a good ab workout?"

"No, the constant coughing gives me a six-pack, though."

Patrick laughed then covered his mouth with a napkin. Dad shook his head, eyes narrowed. Kristie just looked confused.

"It's to help treat CF," I said slowly. "It shakes my chest, loosening all the phlegm—" Kristie's face reared back and her mouth twisted like I had offered her a boogie sandwich.

"STOP!" Dad bellowed. "Kristie has a delicate stomach. I've tried explaining CF to her in the past, but it makes her nauseous, so let's just stick to other topics. Is that so hard?"

I stared at my plate. I used to think Dad was as smart about CF as Dr. Edwards. He used to be the one to take me to all my appointments and tell me about all the new treatments that were being developed. In fact, that's what Mom and Dad used to fight about most—late at night when they thought I couldn't hear. One time, about a year before Dad left, Mom yelled that he had to face reality and stop raising my hopes. He shouted back that if he didn't have hope what did he have? "Caleb!" Mom had screeched.

"That's not enough," Dad had said. Or maybe he didn't. It was late. All I know is that Dad doesn't research anymore.

And now this. Proof that Dad had never even mentioned my treatments to Kristie. Did he talk about me at all? I peeked around the apartment. Tons of pictures of Kristie and Dad—playing tennis, going sailing, dressed up for some fancy party. Patrick's senior picture (him in a suit) hung on the fridge. There was a framed picture of Kristie's cat, Snickers, who died a couple years before we knew her.

I swallowed a few more pills and downed my shake.

"The salad is really good," Patrick told Kristie.

"Thank you," she murmured.

We all quietly ate—or, in my case, drank—our meals. It wasn't until Patrick kicked me under the table that I realized something was up between Kristie and Dad. It was like two mimes arguing. Kristie kept tilting her head toward us and mouthing *Do it!* Dad kept slashing his hand through the air and mouthing *Later!*

"There something you'd like to tell us?" Patrick asked.

Kristie's eyebrows popped up and she gestured at us. Dad sighed, plastered a giant smile like it was a Band-Aid across his face, and said, "Kristie and I have decided to start a family."

Kristie squealed and clapped her hands. "Isn't that amazing?" She turned to me and Patrick, her smile wobbling again just a bit when she saw we weren't reacting in kind. "You boys are so adorable"— Patrick winced—"I can just imagine a baby with your dad's green eyes and my dark hair!" She squealed again.

"Congratulations," Patrick said.

"Oh, no need for congratulations yet," said Dad, his smile a bit more genuine now. "We've only just started trying. These things take time. The chance that Kristie is actually pregnant is pretty slim. It took months of trying before Steph—"

Kristie cleared her throat, and Dad stopped talking like he swallowed his tongue.

This time, I joined Patrick in the wince. "Too much information, Dad," I muttered.

Kristie giggled. "If it had been up to me, we would've gotten to this point a lot sooner! Your old stick-in-the-mud Dad insisted on genetic testing to make sure I'm not a carrier before we started trying. The news came back last month. I'm perfectly healthy, and our baby will be, too!"

All of this was said super brightly, so lightly. Suddenly, I couldn't see the plate in front of me. Couldn't hear anything but a whooshing pounding in my ears. My heart was beating too fast. My lungs couldn't keep up with the air I tried to pull through them. My throat was closing.

"Are you okay?" Kristie asked.

"He's fine," Dad said. "It's not a big deal, Caleb. We just wanted to be sure."

Yeah, no biggie at all. They were just waiting to have a baby until they could make sure the kid wouldn't turn out like me.

"Nice," Patrick muttered, and threw his fork onto his plate with a rattle.

"I didn't mean—" Kristie started with a shaking voice. I didn't have to look up to know she was crying.

"No, it's okay," Dad told her, comforted *her*. "You didn't do anything wrong."

This time, I did look up. Dad stared right back, his face set. "Come on, Caleb. Don't make a big deal out this. You wouldn't want a baby to go through what you deal with, would you? What you're going to deal with? What we're all going to have to endure?"

I just sat there, like a tree rooted to the spot. Just sat there, staring stupidly back.

Patrick stood. He put his napkin on his seat and pushed in the chair. "Thank you for dinner," he said to Kristie, "but Caleb and I need to be going now."

"Don't be like that," Dad growled. "You're hurting Kristie's feelings."

"Maybe *I'm* not the one who needs some lessons on sensitivity." This time my gasp had nothing to do with my own panic. Patrick *never* talked back to Mom or Dad.

"Come on, Patrick!" Dad stormed, standing now, too. "Taking lessons from your mom, I see. You sound just like her."

"Too bad you can't seem to hear us!" Patrick shouted right back.

Part of me was fascinated. Perfect Patrick never lost his cool. But mostly I was trying not to totally lose my own control. *One, two, three* . . . I counted. But the more they screamed at each other, the harder it was to concentrate. *Four, five.* Breathe out. *One, two, threefour-five!* My heart slammed against my ribs. I scratched at my throat. I couldn't sit there! I couldn't breathe here!

"What's wrong with him now?" asked Dad, distracted by my flailing.

Patrick's voice lowered. "He's having a panic attack."

Dad's arms flew up and flapped down on his legs. "A panic attack? Seriously?" He sat back down and buried his face in his hands. "Kid can't even cry without it being a medical condition."

I jumped up from my seat and realized I didn't have anywhere to go—I didn't even have a bedroom here, just Kristie and Dad's spare room with its double bed and nothing else. Soon, I guessed, it'd be a nursery. I turned and rushed out the front door.

"Caleb!" Dad shouted. "Get back here!"

"Leave him alone," Patrick said as I let the door slam behind me and sunk to the front stoop.

⤞⟩⟩⟩⟨⟨⟨⤛

About ten minutes passed before I realized Patrick was beside me. Maybe he had just come outside or maybe he had been there all along. I didn't say anything, just nodded when he handed me my backpack and slid his own up his arm. "Ready to go?" he asked. I followed him down the sidewalk. It was still light out. The two-mile walk home took us almost an hour. We didn't speak the whole way.

When Patrick unlocked the front door, I tossed my backpack inside and went straight to the bathroom. When I felt normal again, I headed to the front door.

"Where are you going?" Patrick asked.

"For a walk."

"We just took a really big one," Patrick pointed out.

"I'm going for another."

"In the woods?"

I nodded. I was just a few feet into the trees when I heard music, angry and fast, pulsing from Patrick's violin and out of the house.

❧ ⚜ ☙

Kit wasn't waiting on Mermaid Rock.

I kicked off my sneakers, tucked my socks inside, and left them on a rock, then I stepped barefoot across the stream. It only went up to a couple inches above my ankles, but it was cool and perfect after the long walk from my dad's house.

On the other side of the stream, I picked my way through the woods to Kit's house. I kind of smiled to myself at how clear the trail looked now—straight to the hollow tree, through the honeysuckle patch, slight right between the pines—compared to a week ago when I was totally lost.

At first, I thought maybe Kit wasn't home. No lights were on in the house. I didn't hear any sound at all. But as I got closer, I heard a *swish-swish* coming from the front porch.

There on the step was Kit, dipping a paintbrush into an old can and spreading a thick layer of rusty red on the wooden porch. She must've started by the door since the only thing left to paint, aside from the steps, was a patch of faded green around her body.

"What are you doing?" I asked.

Kit didn't turn around, her hand just paused midswipe. "Tap dancing with chickens."

I guess it had been a pretty obvious question. "It, um, looks nice."

Kit laughed, still not turning around. Truth was, it did *not* look nice. The red was dripping and thick in some places, barely there in others. Worst of all, Kit hadn't done anything about the huge peeling chunks of old paint—just brushed right over them. So even though it was freshly painted, it still looked old.

She finished her Kit-size empty blot of space by standing on the stoop and swishing over it with the paintbrush. "I found this paint in one of the outbuildings. I couldn't let it go to waste!" She stepped back, placing her bloody-looking hands on her hips, even though it stained her T-shirt and shorts. She scanned over her work. "It looks like someone slaughtered a cat."

"And then twirled its headless body in the air a couple of times," I added without thinking. But Kit just laughed.

"Isn't your mom going to get mad that you did this?" I said.

"Nah, she won't care. My mom's big on independence." For the first time since I got there, Kit turned around to face me.

"Kit! What happened?" A bruise spread across her face, from her cheek to jaw bone. It was dusky blue, with red around the edges. When she reached up to touch it with painted-red fingers, I spotted smaller scrapes and bruises down her forearm. "Are you okay?"

She grinned, rolling her eyes. "It's nothing. I tried climbing one of the pine trees and a limb snapped. My face smashed into the trunk on the way down. I'm fine."

"Are you sure? It looks—"

"I said I'm fine," said Kit, not smiling now. "Can we move on?"

"Yeah, sorry." I shoved my hands into my pockets.

"I'd offer you a drink of water or something but we're sort of painted out of the house," she said. "Race you to Mermaid Rock?"

<hr>

We sat on the rock as the sun dipped lower in the sky. "Think the paint's dry yet?" she asked.

"Probably not," I said, but only because I didn't want her to leave.

I had just finished telling her how much I hated camp—how stupid it was. Now *I* was feeling a little stupid. Kit had said to stop going, as if that were an option. And I knew, without a doubt, that it would be an option for her. I knew she was sick of talking about it.

My phone buzzed with another text from Patrick. I quickly knocked out a message to him: *Be back by dark.*

Kit grabbed my hand as I was about to shove my phone back into my pocket. She put the phone beside us on the rock and flattened my hand, palm side up, on her leg. She leaned forward and squinted at it. I tried to pull my hand away. The tops of my fingers are too thick and flat. But Kit yanked back, holding my hand in place.

"When I was rooting through Grandmom Ophelia's old stuff, I didn't just find paint. I also found a stack of tarot cards. I did more digging, and it turns out that I am a descendent of the great Ophelia Root, seer of the unknown!" She pulled my hand closer to her face, running a finger along its lines. "I can see your future!"

"Whatever," I said. I couldn't tell if this was another of Kit's stories. Her face was set, the bruised side in shadow, making her pale blue eyes look mysterious. Clouds drifted in front of the setting sun, making her hair look even darker. Firefly glows peppered the air around us. The setting sun cast a beam of orangey light straight onto Kit and across my palm. My arms broke out in chills.

I pulled back my hand but she squeezed her grip.

She poked the hollow in the middle of my palm, muttering something under her breath. "The spirits are speaking to me!" I yanked my hand back as the woods around us erupted in a chorus of calls from birds roosting in the trees. All at once, they took to the sky like a polka-dotted black cloud. Kit's eyes widened to perfect circles. She tilted her head to the side, as if hearing a conversation even though all I heard were birds.

"I don't want to know—"

"The spirits say," Kit interrupted in a high, quaking voice, and, I swear, all the birds quieted at once, "that you are destined for greatness beyond the confines of a park summer camp!"

I laughed. "Do the voices tell you how I'm supposed to get out of it?"

Kit squinted, shifting my hand toward the last bits of sunlight. "Ahh . . . ," she drawled out the word. "It says here your days would be better spent with a new friend, one . . . oh, I see it . . . who is destined to be your best friend."

Brad's face popped into my head for just a second, but then all I saw was Kit as she kept reading my palm. "It says here that you'll figure out a way to spend summer days living your life the way it was meant—no, I say, decreed! With me!"

"Are you sure you know what you're doing?" I laughed. "Because I'm pretty sure Mom decreed I spend summer at camp."

"The fates disagree," Kit said. She tilted her face to the sky as a single blackbird soared. "Don't you agree?" she called up to it. The crow screeched. "See?" Kit smiled back at me as if the bird answered any remaining doubt.

Kit still cradled my hand. I realized my palm was sweaty and gross. But Kit's grip tightened again before I could pull it away. "I'm not finished with my reading."

"I don't want to know my future."

"Silence!" Kit said in a spooky voice. The crow called out again, as if it, too, was scolding me. Kit's finger traced the line that ran from below my thumb to my pointer finger. Her touch was super light but somehow it stung like a bug bite anyway. "This is your lifeline," she murmured. She squinted at it. "It's—"

My phone buzzed again, making both of us jump. "Okay, okay!" I said to the phone as much as to Kit. "I've got to go." I slipped off the rock and shoved my phone in my back pocket.

"See you in the morning!" Kit said as I pulled on my shoes and socks at the shore.

"Maybe," I hedged. I turned around to face her, still perched on the rock. She looked as pink and gold as the setting sun.

"Definitely!" she called. "It's destiny! You can't fight destiny."

⤙⤜⤙⤜

Patrick stood by the door, arms crossed, as I rushed through. He sighed and I'm sure he was rolling his eyes, but I dodged pass him. "It's seven fifty-eight!" he stormed.

"I know!" I shouted back. "I was having fun, all right?" I snatched the meds and my nebulizer from the counter and darted back to my room.

Patrick didn't say anything else or follow me. I shimmied into the vest and plugged it in, turning on the nebulizer. I held the phone on my lap, waiting for Mom's inevitable phone call. Five minutes later, the nebulizer mostly zapped, my phone buzzed with an incoming FaceTime call from Mom.

"Caleb?" she asked. I saw her eyes swiping across the background, taking in that I was, in fact, doing my routine. She smiled, her lips shiny with gloss again.

"Hi, Mom," I said. Like her, I was taking in the background more than her face. The lighting was dim, even though people rushed around her. I realized they were all wearing white shirts and aprons. "Are you in a restaurant kitchen?"

Mom's cheeks turned a darker pink. "I'm outside of the kitchen, not in it."

I didn't point out that dental hygienist meetings are generally not held in restaurants. "Having fun?" I asked instead.

Mom's smile stretched and her blush spread. "Yes," she said quietly.

I knew she was watching my face for some sort of reaction. But the truth was, I didn't feel anything. I just ran my thumbnail against the lifeline on my palm, back and forth.

CHAPTER SIX

Mom stumbled into my room just before five in the morning, tying her bathrobe around her waist midyawn. "I got a late start," she said without opening her eyes. "I'm going to need you to get rolling, Caleb."

"No problem!" I grinned when she finally looked at me and saw I already was dressed. I had on the Wednesday camp T-shirt (electric pink) with my favorite Captain America T-shirt hidden underneath for a boost of courage. I buckled my vest and set up the nebulizer, snapping the pieces into place.

"When—how . . ." Mom's eyes were wide and her mouth gaped a little.

"I got up early. Set my alarm." I flipped the switch to turn on the nebulizer and popped it in my mouth. I pressed play on the remote and pretended this wasn't a big deal.

"Oh," Mom said, smiling now. "Great."

By the time Mom got out of her shower, I was ready to go.

"Do you have your meds packed?" Mom asked. I held up the pill box for her to inspect. She nodded, that little smile still on her face. "What about your lunch?"

"In my backpack with two ice packs. I also grabbed sunscreen and bug spray."

Instead of heading to the door, Mom pulled out a chair at the kitchen table and gestured for me to sit. She sank into the one beside me. Across from us, Patrick curled over his cereal bowl. He had another hour to go before his internship started.

"What is this about?" Mom asked.

"What?" I crossed my arms and smiled. "You're always after me to be more independent. So, I'm doing it."

Mom folded her hands on the table. "Does this have anything to do with my . . . project . . . last night?"

"Oh, your date?" I asked. Patrick choked on his Cheerios. Guess Perfect Patrick hadn't noticed Mom's lip gloss.

Mom's face flushed as she nodded. "Yes, my date." Patrick coughed again.

"Nope," I said, still smiling. "It's me, being independent."

Mom's eyes studied my face for a full minute. "What do you want?"

"Nothing," I said.

Mom just stared.

"As part of being independent, I'm going to walk to camp from now on," I said. "It's less than a mile away, and Dr. Edwards said exercise is good for me. I'll leave when you do and I'll walk home every afternoon at three."

Mom crossed her arms. "By yourself?"

"Yes."

Patrick's spoon hovered midway between the bowl and his mouth. Mom pushed out her bottom lip and nodded.

"Are you sure that's a good idea?" Patrick asked. "Maybe you should ask Ava to—"

I fought to keep my voice light, even though Patrick was a total jerkface for butting his stupid self into a conversation that had nothing to do with him. "I'll have my cell phone on me the whole day. Mom can check on me whenever she wants."

Mom stood, cutting off whatever nosy stupid thing Patrick would've said next. "I'm proud of you," she said, and ran her fingertips through my hair.

I was proud of myself, too, for convincing her. I walked with Mom to the end of the driveway. I kept going down the sidewalk long after her car disappeared around the corner, counting on Patrick to be spying from the front window.

About three blocks away from home, I doubled back, darting through the dewy grass in an old couple's backyard to the edge of the woods. I walked just inside the tree line so I wouldn't get lost until I was back at my house. Crouching down, I surveyed the scene, eyes narrowed on our windows, making sure Patrick wasn't peeking out. The curtains didn't move. I took a deep breath and turned my back to the house toward Mermaid Rock.

-»»».«««-

I figured I'd be alone for a while, waiting for Kit to wake up and head outside. I mean, who willingly woke up at seven in the morning on a summer day? But there she was, sitting on the rock. She had a thick blanket wrapped around her body. Her knees were pulled up so that her chin rested on top of them, and she stared out over the water.

"Kit?" She didn't look up when I called her name. For a moment, I thought she was asleep. "I knew you'd be here." Kit shifted over to make room on the rock while I took off my shoes and socks at the water's edge. When she did, I saw she was wearing the same red-paint-splotched clothes as the night before.

"Did you sleep here?" I asked.

Kit shrugged. "I like the stars."

"You slept on this rock?" I asked. Now that I was closer to her, I saw dark circles under her eyes, merging with the bruise across her cheek. "Your mom let you do that?"

And here *I* was proud that my mom allowed me to walk a few blocks on my own.

Kit groaned. "You are so obsessed with rules all the time!" She shifted so her knees were under her body. Leaning forward, she grabbed my face and held it in place so her crystal eyes were just a few inches from mine. *"Do what you want,"* she said in the same drawn-out, spooky voice she used for telling my future. Her breath was stale and warm across my cheek.

"Do what you want," I repeated. I smiled, feeling my cheeks chunk up because of her hold on my face.

"You look ridiculous," she said. "I think it's got to be the first time you've ever looked fat."

"I do what I want," I repeated, and grinned even wider until she cracked up.

⟿⟩⟩⟩⟩⟨⟨⟨⟨⟵

Kit knelt across from me, two lines of blackish mud smeared under her eyes. The pebbly dirt beside the stream cut into my knees, but I held firm to my position.

"Are you ready," she growled, "for . . . *war*?"

With battle cries erupting from our chests, we unleashed our armies!

Seven gray and red crawfish, pinchers snapping, left Kit's grip. Mine was an army of one—a fat, clammy-skinned toad. I needed both hands to hold him and when I pulled back my fingers, Fred (that was the toad's name) let loose his first weapon. He peed all over my hands, which dripped down over the crawfish. Then, super slowly, he hopped from my hands to land with a lazy plop in the middle of the crawfish. All seven of them turned at once and shot toward the water.

"Huh," Kit said after a pause.

I rinsed my hands in the water. "I'm getting hungry. Want to have some lunch?" Catching the crawfish and the toad, plus turning the woods into a kingdom at war, had taken hours. I had skipped eating a snack earlier, too caught up in building our armies. Mom would've been so mad. *Mom will never know*, I reminded myself. *I do what I want*. Besides, Kit had been here all night and hadn't even had breakfast yet. I felt stupid whining about not having had anything to eat for a couple hours.

Kit shrugged. "Sure." But she didn't move from the rock.

"Should we go back to your place?" I prodded. "I mean, I packed my lunch since Mom thinks I'm at camp . . ."

After a long pause, Kit replied, "Sure."

She skipped ahead on the trail to her house. I tried to keep up, but she disappeared in the forest ahead while I halted to put on my shoes.

"Kit!" I called when I couldn't spot her. "Kit?" I called out every few feet, but she was gone, swallowed up by the woods. Even the blackbird that always seemed to be around, soaring over wherever Kit was, had disappeared.

My stomach rumbled and I knew it wasn't just because I was

hungry. "Kit?" I called, a little quieter. Maybe she had run ahead because she was done hanging out for the day. Maybe she wanted to have lunch at her house alone.

Maybe she didn't want me to be at her house.

"Cah!" The crow landed on the tree branch above me. Its screech made me jump.

"Be quiet, bird," I whispered.

"Cah!" it called, louder than before.

Just then I heard rustling, crashing, through the branches ahead of me. From the side of the woods burst a bear!

Not really. It was just Kit. But for a second, I really had thought it was a bear barreling toward me. It was like her imagination was a virus I caught or something.

She held up a box of cereal—the sugary kind that tastes like cinnamon toast that most moms say no to but my mom's all about getting me to eat as much as possible. "Lunch!" Kit said, shaking the box.

"You're having cereal for lunch?"

"Yeah, why not? Who says cereal has to be a morning only thing? I love cereal!"

"Me too," I said. "Do you want to grab milk or anything?"

"Nah, straight from the box is fine for me." Kit pushed past me back toward the stream. Her hand was already buried in the box, grabbing handfuls at a time.

"Why'd you run ahead like that? Did you not want me to be at your house?"

Kit didn't turn around. "It's too nice to be inside."

I pushed down a briar branch with my leg and stepped over it. "It wasn't that you don't want me at your house, then?"

"Why are you so nosy?" Kit's voice was hard.

"Is your mom home?" I blurted.

"She's sleeping, okay?" Kit threw her hand in the air like I was such a pain in the butt. A few pieces of cereal flew out of her grip and landed off the path. The blackbird swooped down and scooped up a morsel, screeched, and took off again.

"It's just, your mom's never been home before. I thought maybe—"

Kit turned around, and it was so sudden I ran right into her. "It's not like you're so eager to introduce me to *your* parents." Her eyes were narrowed to icy slits.

I bit my lip. She was right. I *didn't* want Mom to know Kit. I dropped Kit's steady glare. If Mom knew about Kit, she'd want to meet her mom. She'd want to invite them over for dinner, or she'd make some sort of basket full of stuff she bought at the bakery and wrapped in her own plastic wrap and "just pop over." She'd see the peeling paint and blood-red porch and she'd miss the turret and the blackbird. She'd ask too many questions and her forehead would crinkle like a dozen frowns over her eyes.

99

I closed my eyes, picturing it all. How would Kit's mom see me? Her kid is shiny and brave, like a balloon just before bursting. She climbs trees and shakes off the fall. She sings and birds answer. How would her mom see me? She wouldn't. She'd see someone boring and plain, skinny and flat. Her forehead probably wouldn't frown, but her eyes—I bet they're the same ice blue as Kit's—would glaze over to something, anything, more interesting.

"I just think it'd be cooler if *we* could just be friends, you know," Kit said a little softer.

We made our way back to the rock to eat our lunches. Kit whistled to the blackbird and it soared over us. She threw a piece of her cereal to it, but the bird didn't catch the food. The blackbird waited for the cereal to drop and then seized it. "Soon it'll eat from my hand," Kit promised.

I was glad she was in front of me and didn't see me shudder. Something about the bird scared me.

Finally, back on our rock, Kit sat cross-legged to eat the cereal. I unzipped my backpack to get out my huge lunch box and Creon tablets. I added a layer of potato chips to my ham sandwich, licking a bit of mayo that crept from the side.

As I bit down, I realized I didn't hear Kit's steady crunching of cereal. "Um, you want some?" I asked around the sandwich.

Her eyebrow popped up. "Do you think you have enough?"

"Har har," I said. "What do you want? I've got carrots and

guacamole, a couple granola bars—the good ones, with peanut butter and chocolate—apple slices with cinnamon, and"—I paused to root to the bottom of the bag—"some Oreos."

Kit shook the box of cereal. "No, I'm good."

But when I made a big deal out of being stuffed, she tore into the cookies and apples. She ate the fruit all the way to the peel, which she left in a circle on the rock with a few pieces of cereal in the middle for the bird.

"That bird, it's starting to follow you around," I said. "Do you know what you're going to do when you catch it?"

Kit grinned. "Actually, I don't think I'm going to catch it after all." Her face had this look—eyes and mouth round as pebbles—that she got when she was piecing together a new game for us. "As it turns out, when I was looking through Grandmom Ophelia's old things, I discovered something else, too."

"Oh, yeah?" I didn't mean to sound sarcastic but saw the flash of hurt on her face. I worked on making my own face blank and open, like hers. I leaned in. "What did you discover from . . . the great seer of the unknown?"

Kit smiled again and I breathed out. "Our abilities come from the fay."

"The what?"

"Fay, silly!" Kit turned back to her crow offering. "It's missing something," she said to herself. She bent and picked a shiny stone from beside Mermaid Rock. After wiping it dry on her shirt, she placed the ruby-red rock in the middle of the fruit and cereal ring. "That's better."

"What is the fay?" I asked. My cheeks were probably the same color as the apple peels. I hate not knowing what everyone else does.

Kit faced me, but her eyes trailed along the treetops like she was looking for a spy. Her voice lowered. "The fay are fairies," she whispered.

"Like Tinker Bell?"

"No, elves and pixies, brownies and kelpies, wisps and wraiths." She leaned into me as she whispered, her breath sour-sweet from the cereal, her hair tickling my face. "Watch out!" she suddenly gasped and pointed behind me. I twisted my head to see the crow swooping above. It landed on a branch across from us, fluffing its feathers and letting its mouth gape with unspoken threats.

Against my ear, Kit whispered, "I think he's a scout for the queen, Titania. She knows I'm a descendent of one of her daughters. The bird is probably Puck in disguise."

There were moments when Kit created these new made-up worlds—of mermaids and sailors, fay queens and scouts—when I was too stiff. Nothing but a body, skin and bone, that refused to see anything but what was in front of me, even as she stood there knit entirely of imagination.

I thought about how Brad would bust on me about this. How

102

Mom would squeal and say something horrible like, "It's so *cute* to see you play." How Dad would sigh. For a moment they slouched and squealed and glared inside my head. I closed my eyes, not that it made a difference. But I wanted to be like Kit, to see stories everywhere. I wanted to make up a new world, one where I wasn't sick and she was magic. I wanted that more than anything. *I do what I want*, I told them in my head. Only I guess I muttered it out loud, too, because Kit grabbed my wrist and quietly asked, "What?"

And suddenly, they were gone. Only Kit was there. I glanced at the bird and, I swear, it glimmered. For a moment, it glimmered and maybe, maybe it even had a monocle. "Did you see that?" I gasped.

"What?" Kit's eyes were circles.

"Hang on!" I said, and sloshed to the far side of the stream where I had spotted it earlier—a chunk of peeling bark from a dying tree. It was as long as my forearm and kind of round. I wrenched it from the tree, planting my leg against the trunk to pull it free. A piece of the bark bent backward, revealing the smooth underside. It was just the size for my hand to grip it. I held the bark in front of me. "Behind my shield," I called to Kit, who still stood by Mermaid Rock. "It'll protect us from anything watching!"

⤛⤜⤛⤜

Close to three o'clock, I jumped over fallen logs and kicked rocks through the woods toward camp. I wasn't sure what time Patrick would take the bus home from his internship, but the bus would pass by the route I *should* be taking home. I knew he'd be looking for me.

I crouched at the edge of the woods—I figured it'd be reasonable to assume it took me a few minutes to get to the woods' edge—and then darted out to the sidewalk when there weren't any cars or buses approaching. Then, realizing I was still holding my shield, I ran back to the woods again. I stashed it in the hollow of a tree.

Back on the sidewalk, I skipped a bit as I walked home. Not a big *Wizard of Oz*–style skip or anything; just a bouncy walk. *I do what I want.* The sentence echoed through my head like an earworm. *I do what I want.*

I smiled and, okay, skipped a little, because here's the thing: I had never spent an entire day doing what I wanted.

Kit's mom was at the house all morning, but never once tromped through the woods or called from the front porch for her. Her mom hadn't even called out before leaving for work. When Kit and I sneaked through the woods to the outskirts of the house after lunch, her mom's little VW bug wasn't in the dirt driveway anymore. I was pretty sure that was a miracle—I'm not sure how much longer I would've made it in the woods without plumbing. (Thankfully, Kit had stayed outside to pile stones into what she called fairy huts while I used the bathroom and then pried open the window and fanned out the fumes.) Kit's house was dark; the only lights were from tall lamps in the corners, and the floors were covered in boxes and piles of bags. Kit had pointed out the rooms on the way to the bathroom. "This one's the parlor," she had said as we passed a room with a huge fireplace and walls decked out in dark wood. But the chairs were still covered in sheets like no one was actually living there yet. It was like they hadn't actually moved in.

My mom, who lost her mind if someone so much as left a damp towel on the floor, had texted a bunch of times during the day. *I assume you made it to camp ok* was the first message. I wrote back, *Yes.* Because it was true. She *had* assumed I made it to camp okay. Around lunchtime, she texted again. *Hope you're enjoying your sandwich! Xoxo.* I texted back: *Yes.* An hour later, she texted yet again. *Don't forget sunscreen!* I texted back another *Yes.* When my phone buzzed again an hour after that (*Don't be afraid to let Ava know if you need to sit out an activity. It's hot today!*), Kit groaned. "Aren't you sick of that? Just tell her to leave you alone!"

I shoved the phone into my pocket without replying. "She just worries about me."

Kit leveled me, turning her eyes to slivers of ice. "You're not a baby. Why do you let her treat you like one?"

"You don't understand," I mumbled. I hadn't exactly told Kit about having CF. I coughed a lot during the day, but she didn't mention it or say anything about the pills I swallowed with lunch. I liked that about her. She treated me like I was normal, just like her.

Aside from Mom's texts interrupting our time together, no one was overseeing us, directing what we did or telling us when it was time to stop or start something else. It was just Caleb and Kit.

Kit didn't have anyone bothering her. Her mom just let her be. How cool would it be to have a life like that, where every day was like this? Where each morning you could figure out exactly what you wanted to do and then just do it?

When I got to the driveway and spotted the curtains flick back, I realized Patrick was watching for me (and, I didn't doubt, the clock); my skipping stopped. The smile faded from my face.

My phone buzzed in my pocket. *Make it home ok?* Mom texted.

I thumbed back, *Yes.*

Another buzz. *I'm proud of you!*

CHAPTER SEVEN

That Friday, Mom came in my room about halfway through my nightly physio routine. She sort of flitted around, checking the nebulizer and the vest, then sat on the bed. For a second, she leaned back like she might lie down beside me the way she used to when I was younger. I raised an eyebrow at her and her back straightened again.

"What?" The word was garbled through my nebulizer mask.

Since I had actually gone to camp—first time since Tuesday—and she was sort of smiling at me, I was pretty sure she wasn't there because I was in trouble.

The day had stunk, too. A lifeguard spotted a toddler pooping in the pool, and we all had to evacuate the water. We spent the rest of the day playing kickball at the baseball field. I mean, most kids played kickball. Ava didn't question when I said I wanted to sit in the dugout.

She had assumed I hadn't been to camp because I was sick, and I hadn't corrected her. And, okay, I didn't sit in the dugout. I sat under the benches of the dugout. From there, I could watch Brad and his dad setting off little homemade rockets in the other field.

"Why are you hiding from Brad?" Shelly had sneered. "Isn't he, like, your best friend?"

"Why are you here at all?" I snapped back. "Is it because, like, you don't have *any* friends?"

I pushed aside thoughts about Shelly and camp, and shook the nebulizer container to see how much more time I needed under the mask. Already I could feel rumbling as the muck in my chest loosened.

"Rough day at camp?" Mom asked. "You seemed distracted tonight."

I shrugged. I knew I had to go to camp once in a while if I was going to keep Mom unaware of how I was really spending the summer, but I wondered if Kit missed me as much as I had missed her today. I knew I wouldn't have gone to camp if she hadn't told me her mom was taking her shopping. It was Kit's birthday.

"Can I have an allowance?" I asked, pulling aside the nebulizer mask for a second, instead of answering Mom.

Mom pursed her lips. "If you need anything, I'll get it for you. Just tell me."

I just rolled my eyes.

"What?" Mom asked.

I pulled the mask aside again. "Maybe I don't want to ask to buy stuff. Maybe I just want to do it."

Mom reached over and adjusted the mask so it was flush with my face. "I'll think about it."

As if that would help me get Kit a present. Not that I had any idea what to get her even if I had money to buy it. Or a way to get to the mall.

"I noticed you didn't eat as much of your lunch today," Mom said.

I shrugged again. No need to tell her I actually ate *more* today than I had all week. The past two days, I had just divvied up my monstrous proportions with Kit. She hadn't bothered to bring out the cereal box for lunch. We even had some leftovers for the bird; yesterday it swooped down for my PB&J crust before Kit's hand was a few inches away from placing it on the rock.

I pulled off the mask since the treatment had ended. Mom didn't say anything, just handed me a box of tissues from the other night-stand while I coughed.

"You need a haircut." Mom leaned forward, her hand ruffling my hair. "And your face—it has so many freckles! I've never seen you as tan as you're getting this summer." She smiled, but for some reason, I couldn't smile back. I picked up the book I had pulled from the book-cases lining our hallway and opened it, not looking at her. I was hoping the book would give me ideas for what to get Kit for her birthday.

"You haven't read that book in a long time," Mom said. I could hear the smile in her voice without looking up. "You used to say it scared you."

I didn't tell her but some of the pages still did. The book was one from when Mom was a kid. It was huge—spanning my whole lap—and bound in a rough cream fabric. The cover had glossy gold letters spelling out *The World of Faerie*. Mom lifted the book from my lap and placed it on her own. "This one was always my favorite," she said, turning to a page with a child-size fairy with black hair and blue eyes standing in the middle of a stream. "Hmm," she added. "I never noticed this." Mom pointed to the blackbird perched on a tree just over the fairy's shoulder.

"Me, either," I whispered, my heart thumping. The child? She looked just like Kit. Okay, maybe the girl in the picture had curlier hair and didn't have streaks of reddish gold through the black hue like Kit, but she had the same sort of face. The same crystal eyes. Maybe Grandmom the Seer of the Unknown wasn't just a story.

Mom teetered the book in my lap again, turning back to the page about goblins I had been reading. "Make sure you put this back on the shelf when you're done reading it."

My mom is usually super generous. Like, if Girl Scouts selling cookies stopped by, she'd buy a whole twelve-box case. She barely makes enough money to pay all our bills, but she always puts at least a dollar or two in the donation jars at the grocery store. She volunteers for everything, even working once a month in a free dental clinic so poor families can have clean teeth.

But all generosity stops at the bookshelf. Her books—especially the ones she's kept from when she was a girl—never leave the house. And, believe me, anyone who bends the corner of a page instead of finding a bookmark better look out! Mom's grandmother gave her this book for her birthday when she was nine. It says so in a little note Mom wrote to herself on the inside cover.

I lifted the book a little higher to hide Mom's face.

"I haven't seen much of you lately," she said, and pulled the book down with an outstretched finger.

"I've been here all night."

"Yeah, but for the past week, you've been in your bedroom except for dinnertime. You eat, and you come right back here." She smiled at me. "I think I know what this is about."

Now I sat up. "What?"

"Calm down!" she laughed, and pressed against my chest with her hand so I lay back on the pillows. I crossed my arms, figuring she actually had no idea. She looked way too calm to know I've been skipping camp all week, but my stupid heart shook like my vest was strapped to it still.

Mom shuffled on the bed, sinking in a little more. "I think you've been avoiding me."

"Umpf." I'm not sure what it meant, but that was the noise that somehow escaped my mouth. I couldn't quite look at Mom. She was right—this whole week, as soon as I got home from "camp," I just sort of hung out in my bedroom. At first it was because I was positive I'd get busted at any moment. But lately it was because I was sure if she looked too long at me, she'd see through my skin to my secrets. I mean, sure I've lied to my mom before. Who hasn't? But about stupid things. Like nodding when she asked if I brushed my teeth (which technically isn't even a lie, since at some point I *had* brushed my teeth) or maybe tossing out a bad quiz before she saw the grade. But skipping camp—that was a big secret. The kind that she wouldn't just lecture me about. The kind with consequences. The kind that might mean she wouldn't sit on my bed at night anymore just to smile at me.

I do what I want. I focused on my book. "I kind of want to be alone," I mumbled.

Mom put her hand over mine. I yanked it back, not looking at her.

She cleared her throat, then said, "I think this is about the date I went on last weekend. Ever since then, you've been acting so independent and quiet." She bit her lip. "I appreciate your support; it's more than I could've hoped for and much more than I expected. But just because I'm dating Derek doesn't mean you're even a smidgen less important to me. You're still my priority, and I'll always have time to take care of you." She smiled. "I *like* taking care of you."

"Oh." I flipped the page of my book even though I hadn't focused on a single word. The corners of my eyes stung for no reason. *Sure, Mom. Everything I've done all week is because of you. Because you went on a stupid date. Nothing could be going on in my life, right? Everything's all about you.*

That's what I wanted to say. What I really said was: "Derek, huh?"

"Do you remember him?" Mom asked. She sounded so . . . so girly.

I nodded and flipped another page. A couple times last summer, Dad dropped me off at Mom's office after appointments. (I could count on Dad to drop me off places early just as often as he picked me up late.) The sound of the dentist's drill made my knees watery, so I would sit outside.

I met Derek—this broad man who smelled like grass and looked sort of leathery—then. He's the one who told me the thing about trees, about how if they like each other, they grow in different directions. Derek also crouched beside me and watched a caterpillar nibbling on the edge of a leaf as if it were a soccer game. He told me caterpillars die a lot because kids pick them up and put them down somewhere else. They usually only eat one type of vegetation, so when they can't find that plant again, they starve. I remembered thinking Derek was like a scientist, and maybe the smartest person I had ever met. "He cuts the grass around the dentist's office, right?"

She stiffened a little and crossed her arms. "A bit more than that, Caleb. He owns a landscaping business. He has employees who cut the grass around the office."

"Then how did you end up with him?" I mumbled.

"Sometimes he cuts the grass, too." She laughed. I didn't. "I think

113

you'll be more comfortable if you got to know him a little better. Derek's coming over for dinner tomorrow night, okay?"

I rolled my eyes.

"What?" she asked.

"Did you really just ask me if it was okay? I mean, you've already invited him, haven't you? I'm sure you told Patrick already." A mean gush of satisfaction surged in my chest at Mom's just-slapped-looking face.

"If you want me to cancel—"

"Do what you want, Mom."

She sat there another few seconds while I pretended to read my book. Finally, she got up. At the door, without turning around, she said, "What's going on with you, Caleb? This attitude, it's not you."

I turned off my light and rolled on my side, letting the book slip under my bed. She didn't know me.

-->>><<<-

Saturday morning, I dragged myself out of bed to do my physio routine. It was strange not having to rush to get to camp . . . or to plot how to dodge camp. Kit said she and her mom would spend all weekend celebrating her birthday, so I had no place to be. After finishing with the vest, I plopped down on the couch and grabbed the remote.

"What do you think you're doing?" Mom stomped down the hall, blue plastic gloves on her hands, one of which clutched a roll of paper towels, the other cleaning solution.

"Watching TV," I answered the obvious.

Mom crossed her arms. Bad sign. "I thought about what you said, about wanting an allowance." She dropped the bottle of cleaning stuff and paper towels into my hands.

"Seriously?" I asked.

"Both bathrooms. Don't forget the mirrors." Mom turned and walked back down the hall. "Or the toilets!"

"How much do I get for this?"

"Payment dependent on quality," she said without turning around.

"Can't I do it later? I just want to relax!"

"Work first, play later," drifted to me from the kitchen. "Welcome to the life of a working man!"

"Never mind!" I shouted. "I don't want an allowance."

"Too bad for you." Mom popped her head into the hallway. "I've decided it's good for you."

"Mom!"

"Caleb!"

She ducked back into the kitchen, singing along to the Joni Mitchell music blaring from her phone.

"If this is how you think you're going to get me to like Derek—slaving around the house cleaning for him to come over—you're *so* wrong!"

Mom turned up the music.

Two things.

First: Perfect Patrick did not have perfect aim because there was no way I was solely responsible for the disaster zone in the bathroom.

Second: A nice crisp twenty-dollar bill in my pocket felt pretty awesome.

"I'll take you shopping tomorrow, if you want," Mom said as she handed me the cash.

"That'd be great!" I said. Something unfurled in my chest as I thought about how I'd duck Mom to get Kit a present for her birthday. And it wasn't guilt. I was *excited*, I realized. I liked having parts of me that no one else knew.

"Not going to happen," said Patrick as he strutted by. "We have to go to Dad's tomorrow, don't you remember?"

Excitement squashed.

"Don't you mess up my clean bathroom!" I shouted when I saw where he was headed.

"You sound like me," Mom said with a laugh. She patted my shoulder. "Maybe Kristie will take you shopping."

I rolled my eyes. "Yeah, probably for maternity clothes."

"What?" Mom's hand on my shoulder clenched.

"Don't worry. They won't have a baby until they're sure the baby won't be like me."

"That's good," Mom said under her breath. Her face had that just-slapped expression again.

I shrugged off her grip and charged toward my room.

Mom called after me, "Caleb, I didn't mean it like that! I only meant it's good because they could never handle—" I slammed my door, cutting off her words.

A long time later, she knocked, but I didn't answer. She eased the door open a couple inches and glanced at my TV. "*Captain America* again?" she said. "I don't understand how you can watch the same movie over and over."

I flopped on my side so she couldn't see my face, even though the movie was at my favorite part—when Cap gets the serum and busts out of the machine taller, stronger, and new. I threw the blanket up over my shoulder. I wasn't crying or anything. I just didn't want to see Mom looking at me. "Leave me alone," I groaned into my pillow.

"I gave you an hour instead of ten minutes," she said softly.

I flopped onto my back and stared at the ceiling. "What do you want?"

Mom leaned against the doorframe. "You know what I said came out wrong. I was just surprised to hear your dad was adding to his . . . family." The last word must've been sticky in her throat; she practically had to spit it out. "I don't want to talk badly about your father, but he isn't exactly good at taking care of others and Kristie is so young—"

"Whatever, Mom." I rolled back onto my side. Something hard jabbed at my ribs. It was Mom's book, *The World of Faerie*.

"Is there anything else bothering you? Anything else you want to tell me?" she asked.

I shook my head, still not looking at her.

Mom stood in the doorway a long time without speaking. "Derek's going to be here soon. I expect you up and pleasant." She picked up the remote and shut off the movie.

CHAPTER EIGHT

Derek held a bouquet of flowers. When I threw open the door at his quick *rap, rap, rap*, he thrust them toward me and then yanked them back. "You're not Steph," he said.

I didn't answer, just stepped back to let him inside.

"I bet you get that a lot," Derek said as he passed. He smelled like soap instead of cut grass. The few times I'd seen him he'd been wearing jeans and a T-shirt; he moved stiffly like the khakis and button-down he wore now didn't quite move with him.

"How are you doing, Caleb?" he asked. "Still catching caterpillars?"

Without smiling, I said, "No."

"Ah." Derek rocked on his heels. We stared at each other for a couple minutes. Listen, I wasn't against Mom dating. She deserved to be happy, right? But suddenly having him standing there in the foyer, I hated him. I didn't understand it. I knew it didn't make sense. But I hated him. I hated him as much as I hated Dad. Maybe more.

Perfect Patrick swept in to save the day again. "Hello, Derek. I don't believe we've met," he said, holding out his hand to shake Derek's.

"Patrick, right?" Derek said as he took Patrick's hand. But, judging from how Derek wagged his hand a little after Patrick let go, I got the impression maybe Patrick wasn't entirely sold on this whole Mom-dating thing, either. "Strong grip," Derek muttered.

Mom rushed out then, wiping her hands on a dish towel. "Derek!" she said and then stopped short. "Yellow roses! My favorite! How did you know?"

"Ah, you mentioned them once a while back." Despite his deep tan, Derek's cheeks turned pink as he handed Mom the bouquet.

Mom held the flowers in front of her, staring at them with shining eyes and a huge smile. Then she brought them closer. For a second, I thought she was going to hug them despite the thorns, but instead she buried her nose in the petals of one rose and breathed deeply. "I mentioned them more than a year ago—when you asked what we should plant by the side doors."

Derek shoved his hands in his pockets. "You said yellow rose-bushes, but the others were worried patients would prick themselves."

For a second Mom just stared at Derek with the goofy grin on her face. *Big deal. So he remembered something you said.* But Mom was acting like it was an absolute miracle. "I thought you liked those carnations with blue tips," I said, thinking of the ones made out of tissue paper that had been in a vase in the bathroom since I brought them home for Mother's Day in third grade. "You said they were your favorite."

"Also favorite," Mom clarified, without turning her eyes from Derek.

Patrick cleared his throat. "Do you want me to set the table, Mom?"

"Oh yes!" Mom smiled at the flowers one more time and then turned back to the kitchen. "Follow me, boys. I thought we'd eat on the back deck. It's so lovely outside tonight."

Derek motioned for me to go ahead of him to the kitchen. Mom trimmed the bouquet and put it in a big mason jar. "I'll just pop these back in my bedroom."

"Your bedroom?" Derek glanced at the table.

Cue Perfect Patrick for the explanation. "Standing water, like in a vase, can grow some nasty bacteria and can't be around Caleb."

"I didn't realize," Derek said. "Sorry, Caleb. I wouldn't have brought flowers if I had known."

"It's not a big deal," I cut in. "They're for Mom, not me."

I sat down in front of the bowl of mixed nuts Mom had set on the counter. Next to it was a little container of hummus and pita chips.

A coughing fit hit me just as I swallowed some of the snacks. I tried to cover my mouth—honestly, I did!—but flecks of partly chewed peanut hit the table. Derek grabbed a napkin from the little pile next to the bowls and swiped it up without pausing.

"Wow," Derek said, as he dipped a chip into the hummus. "This looks amazing, Steph."

"Oh, thank you," she said as she glided back in. As if she had made the hummus instead of dumping it into the bowl from a Stop & Shop container. She picked up a tray of grilled chicken breasts. "Let's go have a seat on the deck."

"Can I help?" Derek asked.

"Sure." Mom motioned to the bottle of wine and two glasses next to the hummus. "Pour us some drinks? Boys," she said to me and Patrick, "bring out the platters."

Derek grabbed the glasses in one hand and the bottle in the other and followed Mom outside. Patrick grabbed a huge bowl of pasta salad, overflowing with chunks of cheese, pepperoni, and vegetables. I sighed and grabbed another bowl, this one full of potato salad and topped with more cheese and bacon bits.

Mom laughed all through dinner at Derek's stories about strange things landscaping clients requested—like the one customer who asked that the workers only wear teal and orange because those were her favorite colors, and another who demanded "nothing green" be planted in the yard because it was "overdone."

Mom told stories I had never heard before about her job when she was a teenager, when she took orders for a catalog company, including one about a woman who claimed to be a psychic. "She told me to watch out for ice. No other details! What am I supposed to do with that?"

"Is that why you never take us ice skating?" I blurted, forgetting that I had decided not to talk during dinner.

Mom covered her mouth with her hand while she laughed. Dad once told her she was nothing but teeth when she laughed, and I guess it became a habit to cover it up. Derek reached out and grabbed her hand, squeezing it. "I like seeing your smile," he whispered.

Maybe I didn't hate him entirely.

Mom bit her lip and turned back to me. "Yes, if I'm being honest. That's exactly why!"

Derek dropped his hold on Mom's hand. He folded his napkin and laid it next to his plate. "I have a lake in my backyard. It's perfect for skating. We'll go this winter, if you want."

I nodded and glanced at Patrick. Not that I needed his permission or anything to like the guy, but I wanted to see if he had noticed how much Mom was laughing. But Patrick stared intently into the woods.

Derek noticed, too. "Is there a bear or something, Patrick?"

"No." Patrick shook his head. "For a second I thought I saw a . . . Never mind. It was nothing."

I squinted into the tree line. Was it Kit? That didn't make any sense; I knew she was hanging out with her mom all weekend. *Maybe it's Queen Titania.* I shook my head at the thought.

"Did you see it, too, Caleb?" Mom asked.

"No," I said. "Nothing but trees."

"Cool trees, too," Derek said. "Check out the root systems." Derek stood and walked down the deck stairs to the lawn. He was halfway across the grass before I got up to follow, shuffling quickly to keep up. Derek knelt by a huge maple and ran a hand along where its roots burrowed into the ground. "Look," he said, and pointed to another root crisscrossing it.

"What's so cool about that?" I asked. Derek raised an eyebrow at me. I gulped and tried again. "I mean," I said, in a softer voice, "what makes that special?"

Derek's mouth twitched. "These trees, they're different species. They'd all grow fine on their own, but they grow *better* when their roots coil. They share nutrients." He stood and held out a hand to help hoist me up.

I dropped his hand the moment I stood. Derek continued, "When I studied landscape architecture in college—"

"You went to college?" My face flamed as I realized how rude that sounded.

Derek chuckled. "Yes, landscape architecture is a learned skill. So is owning a business."

"Sorry," I mumbled.

"No worries. You're looking out for your mom." Derek cleared his throat. "Anyway, in college, I learned that for a while landscape architects planted trees far apart, thinking trees each needed space to grow well. But those trees' growth couldn't compare with what's found in a natural forest. We realized this complicated underground network of roots share nutrients, information. Maybe even help trees communicate."

I stopped in place. "Communicate? Trees?"

Derek laughed again. "I know. It sounds crazy, doesn't it? Communicate in the sense that trees seem able and willing to figure out how to support one another. We've learned that trees will, in essence, *feed* stumps after their trunks are chopped or fall down. Without their branches and leaves, these stumps have no business growing—yet neighboring trees will leech their own resources and food to these stumps. I've got to think it's because the damaged tree is hurting and the others somehow sense it. One in the Northwest even began to grow bark thirty years after it was chopped down. How could it be anything but friendship?"

"You told me about that before," I whispered. "About trees being friends. Then you told me trees that like each other bend away from each other."

"Right," Derek said, glancing at the setting sun. "To give each other sunlight. That's true. But the roots—what goes on unseen—they hold on tight."

Sunday morning, my backpack was packed and waiting for me on the kitchen table. Mom whistled as she wiped up breakfast crumbs from the counter. "Your dad will be here in an hour, Caleb!"

"You don't have to be so happy about it," I muttered. I coughed into my elbow and she handed me a tissue, then bent and kissed the top of my head. Her nose wrinkled. "You know to use shampoo when you're washing your hair, right?"

"Yes!" I groaned, even though I totally hadn't used any.

"I'm sure it won't be too bad." Mom squeezed my shoulder. "It's just a few hours."

Patrick slumped into the seat next to mine. He flipped through e-mails on his phone. "Can I have the car?" he asked. "That way Caleb and I can leave whenever we want?"

"Sorry, kiddos," Mom said. "I'm low on gas and don't get paid until Tuesday. I need to have enough fuel to get me to work the next two days."

Patrick sighed. "Let's just hope he doesn't pick us up in that ridiculous—"

Right on cue, Dad pulled into the driveway in Kristie's convertible.

"Oh, joy," I muttered. "They added a pink pinstripe."

A minute later, Dad strolled into the kitchen. "Ah! Coffee!" he exclaimed without saying hello to anyone. Mom, no longer whistling, crossed her arms as he opened the cabinet above the coffee pot and pulled out a mug.

"I'd appreciate it if you would please knock." She turned her back to Dad and continued wiping the counter.

"I'm still paying the mortgage, aren't I? Still my house." Dad turned and took a long swig of the coffee. He grimaced and put down the cup. Mom made the vanilla-flavored stuff now. "Besides," he said, "who else would it be?"

"Mom has a boyfriend," I blurted. "It could've been Derek."

"Caleb!" Mom gasped. Patrick kicked me hard in the shin under the table.

"Derek, huh?" Dad said. "The guy who cuts the grass?"

"He's a landscape architect," I snapped.

Dad snorted and dumped the coffee into the sink. Mom, two angry red blotches on her cheeks, swiped the mug he had left on the counter into the dishwasher. "Beep the horn from now on. The kids will meet you outside. This isn't your house. This isn't your coffee. I'm not your maid."

A second later, her bedroom door slammed shut.

Dad rolled his eyes and clapped his hands. "Let's go."

Behind Dad's back, Patrick's shoulder slammed into mine. "Nice," he muttered.

Before the torture of going to Dad's house, I had the pre-torture of going to Patrick's track meet. Mom was there, too, sitting on the other side of the bleachers. "Can I go say hi to Mom?" I asked.

Dad, arms crossed and eyes narrowed to where Patrick lined up for his first event, bit off his reply. "You saw her an hour ago."

I waved at her from my seat instead, and she blew me a kiss.

Patrick glanced our way when Dad yelled, "Show 'em what you've got, Patrick!"

Across the bleachers, Mom cheered, "Do your best, love!"

Dad's deep sigh drifted over me like a cloud. I shifted in my seat. I hated bleachers. They always made my back cramp up from sitting too stiff or made me curl over my knees like a bug. I rested my head on my legs. My shoelaces were untied, and Dad's foot, his laces tightly double knotted, rested on top of one of my left shoelaces, locking me in place. For some reason, seeing his electric-blue too-cool-for-a-dad sneaker resting on top of my dirty white fraying lace made me think of tree roots. A little to the right of Dad's shoe was a glob of chewed-up Double Bubble. When the horn blew and the race began, he jumped to his feet right onto it. Then I cheered a little, too, just not for Perfect Patrick.

"That's my boy!" Dad whooped at the end of the race, when Patrick, of course, came in first.

When the track meet ended my back ached a little from sitting on the bleachers. I strayed behind Dad as he rushed to the snack shack.

Back when Dad first left home, he and Mom took us to a family counselor who told them it was important for me and Patrick to have traditions and rituals with both parents as we "transitioned into our new normal." Dad took exactly none of that to heart, except that after every race he went to, he bought Patrick a Gatorade.

I rubbed at my back, eyeing the soft pretzels, cans of pop, and packs of candy. "Can I—"

"Did you just participate in a race?" Dad snapped. "Do anything but make sad faces and complain?"

I rolled my eyes instead of answering. A couple seconds later, when Dad was about to pay for the drink, my throat tickled and I coughed into my elbow.

"Nice try," Dad muttered.

"What?"

"Nothing." He didn't look at me, just turned and rushed toward Patrick, who stood with a tight smile on his face, which was glistening with sweat. Dad and I had to slice through a group of girls sending sideways glances my brother's way to get to him. This time, I actually did cough on purpose, to get them to move aside.

Mom was already by Patrick's side, giving him a hug. "You okay?"

she asked me.

"He's fine," Dad answered. "Got you a drink." Dad handed it over like it was a trophy or something. Like the electrolytes and blue dye made up for absentee parenting.

Patrick glanced at me as I coughed again (this time not on purpose) and thrust the bottle to me without taking a sip. "Here."

I pushed it back, even though it was blue and I love the blue kind. "No, you have it. You're the one who just raced. What did I do?" Dad sighed again.

"Have it," Patrick insisted. "I bet your salt levels are low. It's super hot out."

"I forgot," I said as I twisted the cap off. "You're a CF expert now."

Patrick sighed, sounding so much like Dad I sort of thought the family counselor had been on to something. This little tradition had brought them closer together.

"Fine," Dad groaned. "I'll buy another one. Happy?" he said to me.

"I didn't ask—" I started to yell back.

"I brought him a water bottle," Mom butted in, fishing the bottle from her huge purse and handing it to Patrick.

"Great," Dad said as we both gulped down our drinks (and honestly, it did taste awesome), "let's go. Kristie's making us lunch."

"Oh, joy. Lettuce sprigs and lemon juice."

"Caleb!" Both Mom and Dad said together. They stared at each other a second, in shock that I was so rude, probably. (Honestly, I was pretty shocked that the words slipped out of my mouth, too. I could sort of picture Kit laughing, though.) I waited for the earth to shudder and open up or toads to fall from the sky or some other end-of-the-world-is-nigh follow-up to my parents actually being in sync for a moment, even if it was just to be angry at me.

Finally, Mom said, "His attitude has been an issue lately, if you haven't noticed." Then she turned and marched off in the opposite direction.

-》》》.《《《-

"Is that bacon?" I asked as I stepped over the folded down convertible seat onto Dad's driveway. My legs had been practically jammed into my chest to sit back there; for a second or two I thought I must've been delusional from lack of blood flow. No way would Kristie be making bacon. That kale that scientists claim tastes just like bacon? Maybe.

Patrick sniffed the air. "Yeah, I smell it, too."

Dad's mouth twisted a second. "Kristie's cooking brunch."

I followed Patrick into the house. Almost immediately Patrick stopped, making me walk into him. He flashed me a quick grin and stepped aside. The table in front of us was loaded—I mean, just about overflowing—with pancakes, muffins, scrambled eggs, hollandaise sauce, and a heaping platter of crispy, delicious bacon.

"Hi!" Kristie said brightly as she walked in from the kitchen with a bowl full of orange slices. "Come right in and eat. I bet you're hungry, Patrick, after your meet!"

"Wow," I whispered. "This looks amazing!"

Kristie grinned. "Dig in!"

A few minutes later, after I had my third serving of bacon and drowned my fourth pancake in syrup—the good stuff, butter flavored and thick—Perfect Patrick cleared his throat. "Thank you, Kristie, for making this brunch. I know it's not what you typically have and it . . ." His eyes slid toward mine and away. "It's really nice."

Kristie's pretty forehead wrinkled for a second. Her fork, filled with a giant piece of cantaloupe she had dredged through pancake syrup, paused midair. Still looking like someone figuring out a jigsaw puzzle, she scooped up a bit of bacon and popped the whole concoction in her mouth. While still chewing, her eyes widened and floated to me. "Oh," she said. "Right! Caleb."

Dad sighed. His plate was empty except for a few orange slices and a dry pancake. "Do you want syrup?" I asked him to fill the awkward silence. If Kristie wasn't making this huge buffet for me, who was it for?

Dad shook his head. "I don't eat that crap."

Kristie's cheeks flushed and she put down her fork. "Well, boys," she said, but this time the brightness was a little forced, "we have news!"

"I thought we were going to wait," Dad hissed.

"Not for *family*," Kristie hissed back.

"You're pregnant," Patrick said flatly.

Kristie squealed and nodded. "We got the test results a day after you were last here. It's only a month, but we got pregnant right way. Probably even our first official try!"

Patrick coughed.

Kristie laughed. "I'm sorry, it's just, it's hard to believe how quickly life can change. One month and I'm already feeling like . . . like a *mom*." She squealed again and clapped her hands. It was a pretty non-mom thing to do, if you asked me.

"Already feeling cravings, too," Dad said and swiped his hand toward the bounty on the table.

"I'm not hungry anymore." I put my fork down beside my pancake. "May I be excused?"

"Not quite," Dad said. He put his elbows on the table, cradling his chin in his palms. "I know this is a big adjustment, but maybe a congratulations or a question about the due date, a hug for Kristie, maybe? Come on, Caleb. Think of someone other than yourself."

I stared at my lap, waiting for Perfect Patrick to fill in the gaps. "Congratulations," he said, staring straight ahead and not smiling. "May we be excused?"

Dad's hands curled into fists, one of which he slammed onto the table. "No. We're going to finish this meal that Kristie has prepared for us." Kristie jumped but after a second, she carefully cut into another piece of cantaloupe. Patrick was a statue like me for a moment, but then smoothed the napkin back over his lap.

Was I only thinking about myself? Yeah. Probably. I scooted forward and took another bite of pancake. But it was like my body just said, "Nope. No more for us." The bite tickled everything in back of my throat and I realized it—and a bunch of mucus—wasn't going to stay down.

I hacked, feeling the glob move forward a little but not enough. Leaning forward, feeling each cough shove my ribs into my gut, I scrambled for a napkin. Patrick handed one to me.

Vaguely, I saw Kristie stand, one hand on her stomach, the other at her throat. "I can't get sick," she said. "Please stop coughing over the food, Caleb!"

Patrick pounded my back. Not to be mean or shut me up or anything. It sometimes helps. "He's not contagious."

"But it *is* unsanitary," Dad said, also standing now. "Why don't you excuse yourself, Caleb?"

I spit the mucus into the napkin. Finally, I could breathe again.

"You okay?" Patrick murmured at the same time Kristie said, "Oh, that's gross." Her face turned a scary pale color. (Actually, honestly, it looked a lot like what I just spit up.)

Kristie fanned herself with her hand. "I can't handle that. I'm sorry, but I can't handle seeing you coughing like that." She swallowed, and I saw tears in her eyes.

"Everything makes her nauseous right now," said Dad, as he went to the kitchen to get her a glass of water. "Let's all try to be courteous about it."

"Are you serious?" I asked. "Do you think I *wanted* to do that?"

"Of course not," Kristie said. She smiled at Dad and sipped the water, still fanning her face. "It's just, could you leave the room when you cough?"

"I cough all the time," I pointed out. "I'm *supposed* to cough all the time."

Kristie just stared at me. Another tremble in my chest and I realized I'd be hacking again any second. I got up; maybe I *would* make it out of the room in time. Just as I passed Kristie, she whispered, "Thank you."

And, without even thinking about it, I leaned into her, coughing smack-dab right in her face.

CHAPTER NINE

"What is wrong with you?" Patrick matched his pace to mine. It was a few hours later and we were at the mall, which on any other day would've ranked on a suck level next to living in a musical costarring Shelly. But now that I had that crisp twenty-dollar bill in my pocket, I couldn't wipe the huge grin off my face.

If only I could dodge Patrick. He was the one who suggested Dad drop us off at the mall. Kristie hadn't left her bedroom since brunch, not that I cared. What *was* nagging me now was why Patrick had suggested shopping in the first place. It certainly didn't seem like he was in any big hurry to go off and buy stuff, since he was just following me around. "Did Mom tell you I wanted to go to the mall or something?"

Patrick shoved his hands through his hair. "I listen to other people, okay, butthead? I heard you complaining to her about it. You know, listening to other people might be an interesting change of pace for you."

"What is that supposed to mean?"

"I mean maybe being aware of people other than yourself. Like how you talk to Mom and me."

We turned to step onto the down escalator.

"Oh, so now you and Mom are like the same entity?" I back-stepped, squeezing between the mom and toddler just behind us on the belt and took two more steps back onto the main floor. "I have two parents already, Patrick. Get your own life and stop butting into mine," I snarled over my shoulder, knowing Patrick was trapped going down. Now, to find Kit a gift.

━❱❱❱.❰❰❰━

I knew not to stare at the sun because it could make you go blind from all the brightness. But no one warned me that shops for girls were exactly the same. They were all pink or silver or orange. And glittery. Or they had enormous cartoony signs with giant arrows and hearts and, not even kidding here, unicorns. All of them had crazy bright lights. So many lights. And so many sales clerks. I must've walked by a half dozen stores, waiting to find one that wasn't crawling with, well, girls. Most of me wanted to just park next to one of the old men honk-ing snores on a bench and wait for Patrick to find me.

To delay having to actually enter one of the shops, I stopped and

137

bought a soft pretzel and lemonade. But I fingered the money—I was down to $14.53 after the pretzel—and thought about Kit.

For some reason, I kept picturing that box of cereal she had eaten all week. The way she had worn the same red paint–splattered dress two days in a row. I wanted her to have something special. So I ducked my head and barreled inside the store that was orange instead of pink. I held my backpack on my arm like it was Captain America's shield. I'd go straight to the back where maybe they had something Kit-ish (which, at this point, meant anything that didn't look like a rainbow-farting unicorn had thrown up glitter on it).

I paused by a rack of T-shirts. There was a white one with a black-bird on the front. It would've been perfect for Kit except for the outline of glitter on its wings and the fact that a little cartoon cloud with FLY-ING HIGH hung over the bird. I fingered the words. Maybe I could rub them out or something? Great. Now I had glitter covering my fingers. I wiped them on my pants. Now I was wearing sparkly pants.

"That T-shirt is on sale. Only $37.99 today!" This woman—who had to be at least Kristie's age but wore her blue-tipped hair in spiky pigtails—popped out from a rack of sweatpants with words like LOVE and HEART stitched on the butts. "Looking for something for some-one special?" She winked. The sides of her eyes each had a triangle of gemstones. I bet they were glued there. And her eyelashes were blue. For real.

"Um, no," I blurted. "For myself."

"Oh." Spiky Hair nodded. "I think we have larger sizes—"

"I mean, I'm just browsing. Just looking." I barreled past her, eyes down. Toward the back was a table with notebooks and bags and things. Another clerk popped around the corner. "I don't need any help!"

She eased back behind the rack like a fish retreating into a sea anemone.

The back table was stuffed with notebooks. It'd be pretty cool for Kit to have a place to write down all our stories, right? I started to check them out, avoiding the ones with feathers and fur. (Seriously, a ton of them had feathers and fur.) One just had a picture of the ocean, which kind of looked like our stream, I guessed. Only problem: written across it in the same big bubble letters used on the sweatpants' butts was EAT, SLEEP, SURF.

A familiar sigh wafted over me. "The first two apply, but I'm not so sure you're the surfing type. The ocean's pretty far from Missouri."

I turned and found myself inches away from the last person I wanted to see. Shelly Markel.

"What are you doing here?" I blurted.

Shelly raised an eyebrow. "I'm a person who wears girls' clothes. This is a store that sells girls' clothes. What are *you* doing here?"

And that's when the blue-tipped clerk reappeared. "I found that shirt you were admiring in your size!" She held out the blackbird T-shirt.

Shelly's eyebrow disappeared under her bangs.

"You never saw me here," I said, dropping the notebook and rushing from the store.

"Sort of like camp then!" Shelly called to my back.

Of course I bolted out of the store and right into Patrick. "Hey!" He looked from me to the store and back. "What are you doing?"

"Nothing," I said. "Can we just go?"

"Do you need more time at"—he glanced up at the store sign—"Twinkle Dot?"

"No!" I said, sure my face was even brighter than the sign. "I just—I just saw a friend and said hi."

"A friend?" Patrick bent around me, staring into the store. Somehow he wasn't blinded by it. I saw him do a quick salute-like wave and figured Shelly was still in there. "Okay." A tiny smile tugged at his mouth.

"What?"

"Your friend is kind of cute."

"Shelly?" I groaned. "Ohmigod. Stop. Can we just go?"

Patrick scratched at his head with the corner of a small leather-bound notebook. I snatched it from his hand. It was just a little bigger than a paperback novel, the leather as smooth as the pebbles at the bottom of the stream. It was perfect. "Where did you get this?"

Patrick pulled it back from my grip. "I bought it at the bookstore."

"There's a bookstore?"

Patrick nodded. "Are you okay? Do you need a snack or something? You seem a little . . . off."

"I'm fine!" I shouted. But then my lungs trembled and a cough turned into a coughing fit. "Let's go to the bookstore," I said a few seconds later. I wiped at my mouth with a napkin I had shoved in my pocket after eating the pretzel. "Come on!" I tugged on Patrick's arm.

"No time, Caleb." He glanced at his cell phone. "Dad's in the parking lot waiting for us."

⇢⟩⟩⟩⟩⟨⟨⟨⟨⇠

That night, Mom came in just as I was unsnapping my vest. I tried to cover what I had been working on with the edge of my blanket, but Mom's eagle eyes missed nothing.

"What are you doing?" she asked, tilting her head toward the bulge under the blanket.

"Nothing," I said.

"Looks like something."

I shrugged. "It isn't."

But it was. Dad had dropped off Patrick and me at Mom's right after the mall. Not once in the entire thirty-five-minute drive did any of us speak. As soon as we got home, I went right to my bedroom, only coming out for snacks and dinner.

"You've been awfully quiet tonight, locked up here in your room."

"I haven't been locked up," I muttered. I tried to keep my eyes

141

from darting around the room to incriminating evidence—curled scraps of paper under my desk; squeezed-out glue bottle in the trash can; black and red paint, brushes, and bits of ribbon from the craft basket Mom kept in the hallway closet.

"Looks like you've been feeling creative." Mom leaned against the doorframe, crossed her arms, and cocked an eyebrow.

I shrugged. "I'm tired. Good night."

"Oh." Mom straightened. "Let me tuck you in." Mom came forward and pulled back my blankets before I could stop her. Slowly Mom stepped backward with her hand drifting to her mouth.

"It's nothing," I said, staring down at my pathetic attempt to make a notebook. It was just a bunch of printer paper cut in half. The front and back covers were pieces of cardboard with fabric from an old white T-shirt glued over them. I had poked three holes along the sides and used a blue ribbon to hold it all together. Then, on the cover, I had painted a blackbird like the one on the mall shirt, just minus all the glitter and stupid words. At the bottom, in red paint, I had written *We do what we want.*

"It's not nothing," Mom said. She bent her legs to look at the notebook closer but didn't touch it. "It's really cool, Caleb. I didn't know you could paint."

My face flamed so much even my ears burned. "I can't. Not really. The bird looks like a big stupid blob."

Mom smiled and shook her head. "No, it looks amazing. What did you use as reference?"

I stood just behind Mom, so she didn't see as I kicked her *World of Faerie* book under my chair. "Memory, I guess."

"Who is it for?" Mom asked.

"No one!" I said it too fast for her to believe me.

Mom looked at me over her shoulder, her eyes narrowed again and her mouth twitching. She turned and stood so we were just a couple inches from each other. I was pretty much entirely trapped, the chair behind me and the bed behind Mom, who further pinned me in place with those eagle eyes. "Who's it for, Caleb?"

"No one," I whispered, staring at my feet.

She tilted my head up with a finger under my chin. Her voice was soft. "Patrick told me he saw you talking to a friend at the mall today. A girl."

I jerked free from Mom's hold. At any moment my face was going to spontaneously combust—that's how absolutely on fire it was right then. Forget Captain America, now I was archnemesis Red Skull. My number one target for destruction: Perfect Patrick. My jaw clenched so hard I had to practically spit out, "Patrick is pathetic. When's he going to get a life of his own?"

Mom moved her hand to my shoulder, squeezing it. "Patrick loves you. He's worried about you. We all are, honestly. You've been so secretive. What's going on?"

I stepped back as far as I could, the backs of my legs pressed against the chair. "I'm not secretive," I grumbled. "I just want to be left alone."

Mom's hand dropped. Her shoulders rose as she took a deep breath. For some reason, watching her do that made me do the same. Only where she quietly exhaled, I hacked into my elbow. Mom handed me a tissue.

"I've heard I'm a really good listener," she said. "Sometimes it helps to talk things through, especially relationship stuff."

And sometimes it's nobody's business.

"But then again," she said in her forced-brightness voice, "it's not like I know a lot about relationships."

"Obviously." The word ripped from me like a cough. Mom clenched her eyes and mouth like I had sprayed her with poison. I felt like I had.

"Obviously," Mom repeated quietly.

So, of course, I made it so much worse. "Did Patrick also tell you the awesome news?" I snarled out the words. "Kristie's already pregnant."

She left without saying good night.

-》》》.《《《-

Mom was on her way to work when I finished my vest treatment the next morning. My pills were laid out alongside my huge lunch box and bottle of sunscreen, but she didn't leave a note like she normally

144

does. *Whatever,* I told myself. *It's not like she wasn't going to find out about Kristie eventually.*

"I'm heading to the bus stop," Patrick said from the kitchen table, making me jump. Why did he constantly have to be lurking around? "I'll walk with you to camp."

"No, that's okay," I said. "I can go myself."

"But I pass right by it." Patrick dumped his cereal bowl into the sink and washed his hands. "Let's go."

"Fine!" I snapped. I ran back to my room to pack Kit's gift and put on the stupid electric-green camp shirt.

In the early morning light, the gift suddenly looked so stupid. So childish. Like something we'd make at camp. Kit deserved something special. Something awesome. Not just chopped-up notebook pages covered with a ratty old T-shirt. I shoved it into my backpack anyway. Just as I zipped up my bag, I spotted something else. *The World of Faerie.*

"Come on, Caleb! I'm going to miss the bus!" Patrick yelled.

I added the book to my bag.

At the edge of the park, I turned from Patrick. "Bye." It was the first word either of us had spoken on the whole walk.

"Do you know where to go?" Patrick asked.

Cars were pulling into the park but there weren't a lot of kids around. Up by the pavilion, Shelly sat on the grass, scowling at every-one. I glanced back at Patrick, who now had that same little smirk on his face. "Yes." I sighed. "Just go."

"Right," Patrick said. He grinned. "Looks like she's waiting for you."

Sure enough, Shelly now stood, staring right at us.

"Good-*bye*," I snapped.

Patrick snorted and kept walking. I headed up the small hill with the shortest possible steps, praying Ava wouldn't look up from her clipboard where she checked in campers. When Patrick finally turned the corner, I sprinted back down the hill and into the woods on the far side of the park. I looked over my shoulder once. Shelly watched me for a moment and then drifted back down to a seated position.

-»»»·«««-

When I got to Mermaid Rock, Kit was kneeling on top of it, running the edge of a thin, small rock along the side of the boulder. "We have a mission," she said without looking up.

"What?" I dumped my bag and bark shield, kicked off my shoes at the side of the stream, and headed toward her. "What kind of mission?"

Kit nudged another long narrow rock my way with her bare foot.

"Are we skipping stones?" I asked, tossing the rock up and catch-ing it in my hand.

"Sharpen it," Kit said as she scraped the edge of her own rock against the boulder.

When I didn't move right away, she sighed and took the rock back from my hand, sharpening it herself.

"What's going on, Kit?" I glanced around. The same cereal box that she ate from the week before lay on its side at the creek's edge. The open end was facing me; it was empty. Kit was wearing the same dress she had worn on Thursday, dried mud staining the bottom and fresh dirt caking the front. "Are you okay? I mean, how was your birthday?"

"Fine," she said, scraping the stone harder against the rock.

"I thought you said you went on a shopping spree or something."

Kit didn't look up. "No."

"What—"

"No time to talk about unnecessary topics! I've been up for a couple hours, scouting the perimeter for signs of a fay invasion."

"Oh! This is part of the game. Right!" I grinned, but that was wiped clean a second later by Kit's hard glare. For the first time since I had arrived, she stopped sharpening the stone. "I mean, right. Perimeter. Fay."

Kit shoved her hair back from where it plastered against her sweaty forehead. "Go get your shield," she ordered and hopped into the stream. "We'll need it for the rescue mission. Your sandwich, too."

"Rescue?" I knew just which stones to leap onto now and so was back with the shield in just a couple seconds. Instead of picking out just my sandwich, I grabbed my whole backpack. "Who are we rescuing?"

Kit pushed one of the stones into my hand. Her eyes were hard and her face set. "Let's go."

"Who are we rescuing?" I asked again. The rock was heavy in my hand. For some reason, I had this crazy urge to throw it into the stream and go back to camp. I kept thinking of Shelly, watching me as I left and not saying a word. What if I just went back?

"Someone in trouble," Kit finally answered. "One of us."

CHAPTER TEN

"You know how we're destined to be best friends?" Kit said as we made our way through the woods. She moved deliberately, even though there wasn't a trail to follow, and I rushed to keep up. "How I read it on your palm?"

My hand squeezed the rock, the sharpened edges cutting into my hand. "Yeah, what about it?"

"Well, I had the same feeling, the same down-to-my-roots feeling on Friday," Kit said. She glanced back at me, her eyes like shiny blue marbles in her face. It was her storytelling face, only I didn't know who she was telling this one to, me or her. "So I did some exploring, and I found her."

"I thought you spent all day Friday with your mom."

Kit flicked her wrist at the air between us like my words were flies and continued like I hadn't spoken at all. "I've checked on her every day since—a couple times a day—and I know we're supposed to help her, Caleb. We've got to help her!"

"Help who? A kid? And from what?"

"She's not a kid, but she needs help. They have her tied up all the time. All day long, she's outside on a rope. She didn't even have water for hours yesterday!"

"Are you serious?" My mouth went dry. "How—how are we supposed to save someone with sharp rocks? Shouldn't we call the police?" I twisted a little to feel my phone's reassuring pressure against my hip, where it was tucked into my pocket. My chest rumbled, and I coughed into my elbow. The air was thick and soupy, like sludge moving in and out of my nose. Soon it'd rain. I turned toward the woods and coughed when Kit swung back toward the course we were on.

Kit stormed forward the moment I spit into the trees. *Okay*, I told myself. *Maybe this is part of the game. Just a story*. I figured we were about a half mile or less from Mermaid Rock, on Kit's side of the stream. At the edge of where the woods opened to an unfamiliar lawn, Kit ducked low and beckoned for me to do the same. Her face was only a few inches from mine.

When she spoke, her words were so low yet rushed that they were like gnats nipping at my cheeks. Strands of her dark hair had slipped from her ponytail and whirled around her face, tickling my nose. Her eyes were huge, big enough to block the cough I should've let loose, the knot screaming danger in my throat, and the craziness of what she was saying. "I've read about a girl, descended from fay like me, who was transformed into a dog when her beauty and strength offended a fairy. The fairy had never been threatened by a mortal before that day. To look at a picture of the girl, you wouldn't have thought anything was special about her. But when you were *near* her, you just knew. It was like—"

"—like she was the sun," I finished.

"Right!" Kit smiled, and I could finally take a breath. "I think this is that dog. That's why the owners keep her tied up. That's why they can't control her. She needs to be set free to break the curse and be who she's meant to be!"

"Oh," I said, nodding and trying hard to stop from smiling. Relief flooded through me. This *was* just part of the game. "We're talking about a dog. Right. Cool."

Kit's marble eyes blinked once. Twice. "No. We're talking about a *person* trapped in the body of a dog. We're going to save her." I tried not to squint my eyes as she spoke, her hissed words flying at my face. Kit huffed out of her nose, her nostrils flaring. "Are you going to help or not?"

"Just cut the rope so she can run away?" I swallowed, nodded, and, following Kit's example, army crawled closer to the edge of the lawn. And then, as I looked over the lawn, all that relief? *Whoosh.*

Gone. Replaced with heavy bricks of full-out no-way-let's-go-home fear.

Because this wasn't just any dog. In fact, I could sort of see why Kit thought there was a girl trapped in it. A girl could've literally been trapped inside the beast. This was a wolf. Seriously! I was pretty sure it was a wolf. She was mostly black with patches of brown around her face and chest, but maybe some of the brown was from the dirt surrounding her. I wondered if she had dug up all the grass with her endless pacing back and forth at the edge of her rope. The air was humid enough for her fur to smell damp and rotten. Her leash was way too short, only about twenty feet long, when she alone stretched about six if you counted the tail (which I did—it looked more like a furry sword than a tail). I held the flimsy bark shield against my chest, even though I knew it didn't stand a chance against the dog's huge, sharp teeth.

"I've been bringing her food," Kit whispered in my ear, "so she knows we're trustworthy."

"Did you bring any today?" I asked.

Kit shook her head. "I ran out of cereal last night."

"I don't think she's the cereal type."

"I know," Kit whispered, "but it's all I had."

"Okay," I said, pushing away the question of why Kit only had cereal. I had to focus on getting her to let go of this stupid idea without being the one who looked stupid. "I'm pretty sure dogs don't like tuna fish. And that's all I have in my sandwich." I, however, loved tuna fish. "Let's go back. I'll have Mom pack peanut butter or something tomorrow, and we can work out the details of her rescue."

Kit shook her head. "No, she's waited long enough."

The dog turned then, like she heard us. She probably had. I gasped when I saw her eyes—the same crystal blue as Kit's.

"I know, right?" Kit smiled. She had read my thoughts just like a seer of the unknown.

"I think I'm allergic to dogs," I whispered.

Here's the thing: I'm not exactly an animal person. I mean, I don't have anything against them really. I just never was one to want to hang out with them. Never wanted to be a vegetarian, or a veterinarian for that matter. Something about claws and teeth, I guessed. I gulped. "Did you know that wolves have a bite pressure of about twelve hundred pounds? A naturalist came to school for an assembly once and told us about it."

"Yeah, the same guy must've come to my school," she whispered back. "That means the rope must be pretty thick or she would've gnawed through it already. Good thing I sharpened the rocks."

Someone in the house coughed, the noise drifting from an open window. "Someone's home, Kit. We're going to get caught." Or mauled.

"They never come outside," Kit answered. "Once in a while they yell at her to be quiet, but they've never come out. Look!" Kit pointed to two stainless-steel bowls by the back porch. "Her bowl is empty again." The dog snapped at a fly, catching it by jumping (not even kidding here) straight into the air a foot or two.

I bit my lip. "Kit, I don't really like dogs all that much."

"Okay," Kit said, as if I hadn't spoken at all, "here's the plan: I'll distract her by giving her pieces of the sandwich. You crawl around behind and cut the rope."

"And then what?"

"Then she's free." Kit grinned. "And we run."

"I'm not a fast runner. I'm slowest in my grade. And I'm not all that great at cutting, either. Mom cuts up my steak for me." I realized I was stringing excuses into a necklace of shame, but there was no way I was going to creep close enough to cut that rope. If I were that close, I'd be close enough to not worry about giving up my tuna fish sandwich for lunch. I'd *be* lunch.

"Okay." Kit bit off the word, her teeth clenched. "I'll do it. You distract her." Before I could come up with any more excuses, she crawled forward. I said a curse word in my head and hurriedly unzipped my backpack, pulling out the sandwich. The dog spotted Kit first, the fur on her back rising and her lips curling over her massive teeth. A low growl rumbled from her, and I doubled over, coughing in response. Somehow it worked. Now those dog's icy eyes—the same color as Kit's—narrowed on me.

Even though my knees shook and I wasn't entirely sure I wasn't going to pee myself any second, I stood. "Hey there, um, fairy girl," I singsonged in a high-pitched whisper. "Do you like seafood?"

I unwrapped the sandwich from the wax paper Mom had covered it in. The dog's fur settled across her back as she licked her lips and lunged at the edge of her rope toward me, entirely focused on the sandwich. Kit flashed me a thumbs-up and scurried forward. I ripped off a piece of the sandwich and tossed it to the dog. But my stupid shaking arms couldn't throw and it ended up landing with a soft plop of mayo and tuna a foot in front of her. She lunged and growled and strained against the rope, not noticing at all that Kit was now sawing at the other end of it with the edge of her sharpened rock.

I ripped off another piece, bits of tuna fish flying over my shoes, and threw farther this time. Too far. The dog hopped back and gulped the bite in a second flat, making all the tension in the rope go so slack. *Come on!* Kit mouthed at me as she hacked on the slackened rope. It had just been starting to fray, but without the dog's straining, she was barely making an impact. And, I realized, with a rush of panic that made my stomach jump up and knot around my heart, the dog was on to her. It turned toward Kit, with a scary low growl, and crouched low like it was going to lunge at her.

"Doggy!" I yelped. "Here, doggy! More tuna fish!" My stupid fingers couldn't pull at the sandwich right; I ended up flinging about half of it toward the dog, again landing just outside her length of leash. She turned from Kit immediately and strained toward the hunk of food. I noticed then the pull of her ribs against her fur. Kit was right—the dog was desperate. She stretched her nuzzle, her long tongue lapping against the food. She could almost get it, her tongue reaching just the edges. "Good doggy," I murmured as my heart thumped my stomach back down to its rightful place. "Good doggy."

Kit, her dark hair splattered against her sweaty forehead and fingers white where they clasped the rock, had managed to cut halfway through the rope.

The dog lunged again, making the metal spoke that held down the rope strain. This time she managed to get the first clump of sandwich and downed it fast. Then two things happened at once: first, the rope frayed where Kit had been hacking at it so just a few nylon threads held it in place; and, second, the dog licked its chops, eyes on the only remaining tiny clump of tuna fish. And that sandwich was in my hand.

The dog pulled just as Kit was poised for the final hack on the rope. I stilled, totally frozen in place, fear gripping me so tightly I couldn't loosen my grip on the bit of soggy sandwich. "Stop!" The word seemed to rip out of me, just the way I was sure my heart was about to be torn from my body the moment that last thread of nylon tore.

But then I realized that I wasn't the one who screamed. An older man—probably close to my grandpa's age—stood in the doorway, his mouth stretched midscream. He stumbled down the stairs, but he moved slowly, not helped by his bulging stomach and tree trunk legs.

Time felt like a bubble for a second, stretching out, out, out but snapping back and disappearing in an instant. Kit jumped to her feet, the rope sliced through. The dog surged forward, all teeth and growls and claws. I fell backward, straight onto my tailbone, still holding the bit of sandwich. The old man lumbered toward us, cursing and screaming.

And the dog, the dog! She plowed over to me in two long strides, her terrifying mouth stretched wide. Without even the slightest pause, her snout closed over my hand and she pulled the sandwich out of it. Her teeth scraped along my skin but didn't bite or even close around it. All she wanted was the sandwich.

In a flash she was gone, swallowed up by the woods.

And there was Kit, scooping me under the elbow and yanking me up. "Go, Caleb! Run! Run!"

I scrambled to my feet, twisting and rising to my knees with a painful slam first and then lurching forward before even standing to follow the wolf dog into the woods, the old man's bellows echoing off the trees around us.

➤⟫⟫⟪⟪⟪⟪

"We can't go straight back to Mermaid Rock," Kit yelled over her shoulder as we barreled ahead. "The old man might follow our tracks."

"I don't hear him at all." I stopped, gasping, and held on to my knees for a second. My lungs were filled with fire and felt so tight that I couldn't even cough.

"Don't stop!" Kit grabbed my arm and yanked me ahead. "He's following! I know it!"

Both of us jumped a second later when we heard thrashing in the woods behind us.

I forced my legs to move, but a few feet later, I had to stop again. "I can't, Kit!" I gasped. "I have to stop." I rubbed at my chest with my knuckles. Sweat poured down my spine. "I need to rest." Kit's eyes flashed around the woods behind me and then locked on mine. Again, I felt like she saw more than I ever explained about why I couldn't run as long as her and coughed all the time, and she didn't question it.

"Okay," she said. "Just a little farther. We can hide over there." She pointed to an old barn, half of it sunken into the ground, on the border of the tree line. She slipped her arm under my shoulder, and together we made our way to the dilapidated building. At the edge of the woods, Kit stepped in front of me, looking for signs that anyone was nearby. An old white farmhouse stood in the distance, but it didn't look like anyone had actually farmed there for decades. She waved me forward, and we slipped through a gap in the barn wood. I tried to concentrate only on breathing in and out. How much of this tightness in my chest was panic? How much was CF?

The dry barn air smelled like old bread. Dust floated like hazy clouds with any slight movement in the air. Slanted sunshine peeked through cracks in the barn roof. The roof caved in on one side of the barn, over stalls where I guessed horses once lived. Crates toppled over one another in the corners and in the loft. I sat down next to them, my back against the side of the barn, counting as I breathed out *one, two, three* and in *onetwothree*. When I could stretch the exhales and inhales to a count of five (*five is fine*), I realized Kit had scrambled up to the loft.

"Kit!" I jumped to my feet, even though my knees still wobbled. "What are you doing?"

Her head popped over the side of the loft and she smiled down at me. She seemed too bright in the gauzy light of the barn. "I found something!" Kit eased down the side of the loft, slipping so her bare toes found the top of the crate pile. I rushed over to catch her, sure she'd fall as she pulled down a small box. But she didn't. It was stupid of me to think she would; Kit could do anything. And then a flash of her bruised face from when she said she fell out of the tree came back to me and I held out my arms just in case.

Kit laughed at me. "Don't worry, silly goose." She jumped off the crate with the box still in her hands and sunk to the barn floor. "Look what I found!" I sat beside her.

"Listen, Kit," I started to say as she opened the box. "We've got to get out of here. Let's go back to the rock."

"Oh, come on," Kit said. "This barn is a treasure chest. Look!" Kit pulled a blue bottle from the box, rubbing off some of the dust with her shirt. It was small, only about the size of my palm. Bubbling out from the glass was the word SERUM.

"Serum? That's what turned Captain America into a hero." I grabbed the bottle from her. It was the same color as the medicine given to Cap, too. "Huh." I handed it to Kit, who pushed it back toward me.

"Keep it," she said. "It's yours. I can tell."

"I can't keep it. It isn't ours."

A raindrop pelted against the roof of the barn. Kit rolled her eyes. "Look around, Caleb. No one cares about the stuff in here. It's all pushed aside, waiting to be crushed when this roof finally caves."

"It's still stealing, even if no one ever notices." And suddenly the *World of Faerie* book blossomed in my mind. I pulled the strap of my backpack up my shoulder.

More raindrops hammered, sounding like nails being slammed into the old wood over our heads, and the scant sunshine faded. "We should go." I pushed myself up to my feet. My stomach was grumbling. I was going to need to find a bathroom soon. Something else bothered me, too. Like a little mouse gnawing on my gut, something ate away at me. I just couldn't put my finger on what it was.

Kit sighed, slipping the blue bottle into her pocket. Then her hand darted down and grabbed another, almost like it but bigger, and put it in her other pocket. "They'll never miss them. I swear."

Just as we climbed through the broken board, lightning shot

across the darkened sky. Thunder rumbled like a monster's roar a moment later. Kit squealed and ducked back into the barn, dragging me with her. "We can't go out in this."

"But we can't stay here!" I clenched my fist. The scrapes from the dog's teeth weren't deep, barely scratches really, but they stung. I shoved my hand into my pocket, my fist closing around my phone. What if I just called Mom, or even Patrick? Would they come for me? *Don't be stupid*, I told myself. *How would I explain being in a barn with Kit?*

Kit settled back against the barn wall. "This is the perfect spot for a picnic. Let's just eat here." She looked like Shelly when she was the only one who knew the answer to one of Mrs. Richards's math problems in school. That's when it struck me, the thing that had been bothering me all afternoon. School. And it was just like in a cheesy movie—the moment I remembered, a lightning bolt crackled across the sky.

Kit's lips moved as she counted. When thunder boomed, she said, "That was five seconds. The storm is about a mile away. I bet it'll be over in a half hour, max."

"Where did you learn how to do that? Count between lightning and thunder to figure out how far away the storm is?"

Kit paused, her eyes narrowing. "I don't know. I must've picked it up somewhere."

"In homeschooling?"

161

"Yeah," Kit said, and started rummaging through the box again. "In homeschooling."

"Not science class."

"What are you getting at, Caleb?"

I crossed my arms. Goose bumps popped out over my arms and not just because of the storm's drop in temperature. "Before we cut that dog loose, you said you saw the naturalist assembly at your school, too. But when I met you, you told me you had *never* been to school."

Kit sighed. "What's your point?"

"You lied to me!" I sort of yelled.

"So what, okay?" Kit's voice was mellow but stung all the same. "I lied. People lie sometimes."

"But why?" I asked. "It doesn't even make sense. Why would you lie about that?"

Kit shrugged. "It just sort of happened. I mean, I just sort of said it. It didn't make sense to start school when we moved in May, so I just stopped early for the summer. But I *am* going to be home-schooled next year, okay?" She looked up at me, and I saw two pink patches on her cheeks. She felt bad, I could tell, about lying.

The anger nibbling at my gut finally loosened its jaw. It wasn't like I never lied. I could name six times since Tuesday. And she had never pushed me about anything—about why I swallowed a half dozen pills before eating or why I ate enough food for a horse every

162

day. I sat down next to her, my stomach grumbling. I was so tired.

I unpacked what was left of my lunch. Mom always packed me two juice boxes, so I handed one right away to Kit. I downed my pills and spread out the rest of the food. An apple, carrot sticks, two cheese sticks, two granola bars (one labeled *Snack time* in Mom's careful handwriting). Kit divvied them between us, and we ate while rain hammered the roof.

As hungry as I had been a moment earlier, I had a hard time finishing even the cheese stick. I forced it down and ate a couple carrots. Kit hummed under her breath, checking out all the different bottles. Maybe if I lay down, my stomach would settle and I'd be hungry again.

-》》》.《《《-

I hadn't realized I was sleeping until I woke up. I opened my eyes and the air was still and thick and almost vibrating, the way it always is moments after a storm. My stomach clenched but I ignored it, trying to remember what had happened. Did we really set free that dog? I grinned at Kit, who had stopped humming and was watching me. She smiled back and soon we were laughing. It all seemed so funny suddenly—a big adventure.

And then I ruined it with my stupid mouth. "You didn't go shopping with your mom, did you?"

Kit's eyes clouded over the same way the skies had earlier. I held my breath, half expecting that any second I'd see a flash of lightning and need to count seconds. But Kit just grew very still. She looked at the bottle in her hands, this one with notches and numbers along the sides like measurements. "I think these had medicine inside once," she said instead of answering.

I didn't say anything, letting my question swell around us. Finally, she said, "No. She's looking for work—she used to work at a store but quit." Kit shook her head. "That's a lie. She didn't quit. She was fired. She didn't show up to work. After my dad left a couple years ago, she just sort of . . ." Kit tipped the empty bottle, as if pouring out all the contents. "Sort of was empty. She keeps saying she's going to do things and then doesn't. Like she said we'd fix up Grandmom's old house, but it's exactly the same except for the improvements I've made."

I didn't say anything, thinking of the red porch and wondering what else Kit had done.

"Grandmom lived with us for a while. She kept Mama on track, you know, made sure she took her medicine—she gets strange thoughts sometimes—and Grandmom made sure I was okay. Grandmom's the one who told me about the fairies." Kit kind of smiled as she glanced over at me. She tossed me the serum bottle.

"What did she say?" I asked, looking down at my bottle.

"Grandmom said Mama was so beautiful when she was a child, so special, that the fairies couldn't resist playing with her. But since she was human—all the way human—she couldn't handle the contact. It twisted her mind so she sees things humans can't, hears things that aren't there. It's the fairies."

I bit my lip, thinking hard. "It sounds . . . sounds kind of crazy, Kit."

Kit stilled and didn't speak for a long time. "I know it sounds crazy. I'm not explaining it right. But if you could've seen Grandmom when she told me, you'd know. You'd believe her."

I nodded. "You're like that. I believe you, too."

Kit continued as if she hadn't heard me. "Grandmom took Mama to doctors, made sure she took the medicine that kept the fairies from bothering her too much. But now Grandmom's gone. And so is Mama, mostly."

Kit grabbed a different bottle and her hand clenched around it. "She's never even home. She makes promises all the time. 'We're going to go shopping.' 'We're going to go into town.' 'I'm going to sign you up for school.' And then it doesn't happen. She'll come home, later and later, and say she's sorry. Say she'll make it up to me. But she won't. She can't."

I racked my brain trying to think of what to say. But I couldn't think of anything.

Then Kit stiffened and sort of shuddered, like she was throwing off an itchy blanket. When she looked at me, her eyes were fierce as the thunder I had been waiting to hear. "She's constantly doing that, you know?"

"Doing what?" I asked quietly. I focused on the serum bottle, tilting it so it caught glimpses of the sunlight. Kit had taken most of the other bottles out of the boxes and they lay around her in a ring. None of the others were blue like mine.

"Trading her todays for tomorrows. 'I'm sorry, Kit-Kat. I can't today. But tomorrow will be great. Tomorrow will be awesome. Tomorrow I'll make it up to you.' Always *tomorrow*! I'm not like that. I'll *never* be like that." I had to look at Kit then, when her voice snagged on her last words. Kit reared back her arm, throwing a bottle as hard as she could against the barn wall, where it hit with a bang and shattered into dozens of pieces. Then she grabbed fistfuls more of the old bottles, throwing them all against the wall to shatter in showers of forgotten green and clear glass.

Kit did all of this—this eruption of shattering glass—without crying or screaming or moving with anything but purpose. I was frozen in place, too scared, too startled to do anything, even ask her to stop. But the thing that made it even harder for me to move? Kit wasn't sad. Wasn't angry. She was as determined and deliberate as when she told me about our destinies. "I won't trade my todays for tomorrows. I'm going to make every day mine. Every moment of it." Kit stood and pulled the last bottle (aside from the blue one in my own hand) from her pocket. Her fist tightened against it, but instead of throwing it away, she put it back in her pocket. Kit handed me my backpack and nodded toward the opening in the doors. "You can't count on tomorrow. No one can."

Every day mine. The words rattled around my skull.

"I have something for you," I said, and opened my backpack. But the corners of the notebook I made had curled in the humidity. Some of the black paint blurred. I bit my lip and reached behind it. Mom would never notice the book was missing. It wasn't like she read it a lot or anything. It was sort of like the blue serum bottle in my pocket, wasn't it? Just sitting in here, gathering dust instead of being used, having a purpose. I pulled out the *World of Faerie* book and handed it to Kit. "This made me think of you," I said.

She pulled it onto her lap, her eyes wide as she brushed her fingertips across the paintings of fairies. "For me?"

"To keep," I added.

CHAPTER ELEVEN

Something awful happened before I left the barn. Something I don't want to talk about. Something I couldn't help and that Kit, waiting outside for me, pretended not to notice. She's good at pretending.

※

The stream surged after the storm, making tiny rapids around rocks and reaching the middle of our calves. Even though we had stayed mostly dry in the barn, our wet clothes now clung to us thanks to trees dropping raindrops on us at the slightest breeze. What was the point of trying to stay dry, anyway? We stood in the middle of the stream, sending armfuls of water to erupt and shimmer like fireworks as we threw them in the air and over our heads. Nothing mattered then. Not the chill that soaked through me from the storm and its sudden coolness. Not the old man's stretched-out and angry face. Not the stinging scrapes along my hand from the fairy dog. Nothing at all but jumping and splashing and being, totally being, in the moment.

I could still wring rain and stream water from my shirt as I crept to the edge of the park that afternoon. No one spotted me as I made my way to the sidewalk. That's what I thought anyway.

"Hey!" someone yelled behind me.

I whipped around, heart pounding, but it was just Shelly. "Hey," I said and turned back.

"Hold up," she said. I could hear her sneakers hit the sidewalk as she trotted toward me.

"Shouldn't you be up at the pavilion, making Ava's life miserable?" I muttered.

"Shouldn't *you* be?" she said back. "I want to know what's going on." Shelly gathered her frizzy hair into a ponytail and matched my long strides. "I told Ava I was going for a walk, and I'm not going back until I have answers."

"Nothing is going on," I said. "I just don't want to be at camp."

"Caleb," Shelly said in her I-know-everything voice, "*no one* wants to be at camp. But that's where you're supposed to be. Ava thinks you're sick or something."

I didn't say anything.

"Are you sick or something?" she asked quietly. "I mean, I know

you have cystic fibrosis, but you always seem fine to me. A little enti-
tled maybe, but—"

"Back off, Shelly," I snapped.

"Fine, but at least tell me what that's supposed to be." Shelly
pointed to my arm and I felt like a complete dork. I forgot to stash
the shield behind the tree. I couldn't turn back now, not with Shelly
watching me.

"It's vibranium," I muttered. That's what's in Captain America's
shield, not that Shelly would have any idea.

"Come on," she said. If someone could talk in a rolling-your-eyes
tone, that's totally what Shelly was doing. "That shield's not even
adamantium quality."

"Hey—how do you—?"

Shelly's cheeks flared. "I like Captain America. Thought I saw
you reading one of the comics during math class last year."

I didn't say anything for a second. "Who's the better villain—Red
Skull or Crossbones?"

"Neither," she said, this time actually rolling her eyes. "Batroc is
the best."

"Batroc? Are you insane?" I laughed. "He's such a weirdo. A total
joke."

"Oh, please. Batroc and his brigade could destroy Hydra without
getting a single scratch."

"Batroc is lame. All he ever does is kick things."

"Kickbox things," Shelly fired back. "Difference."

"Lame."

"Whatever." She laughed. Shelly's laugh was nice. Soft and musical, not obnoxious like the rest of her. "So, why do you need a shield?"

"I don't—"

But before I could come up with a suitable lie, the bus pulled up and out stepped Perfect Patrick. Never had I been so happy to see him in my whole life. "Patrick!" I yelled. "Okay, gotta go, Shelly. My brother's here. Head back to camp!"

Patrick looked from me to Shelly, Shelly to me. Then he got that stupid smirk on his perfect face again. "That's all right, Caleb. You can hang out with your *gir—*"

"Bye, Shelly!" I yelled over my shoulder, sprinting ahead to Patrick. "See you!"

"Tomorrow, right?" she called back. "At camp?"

"Right. Tomorrow!"

→⫸⫷←

Mom hummed in the kitchen as she made dinner.

"Need some help?" Patrick asked. Part of me wanted to join her the way I used to, chopping up veggies and washing lettuce and laughing at her attempts to dance. But I was so tired from everything that had happened that day, I couldn't muster up the energy to offer.

I slouched on the couch instead and pulled a blanket over

me. I couldn't seem to get warm, even though I had turned off the air-conditioning.

Mom's phone rang and I heard her laughing, high and tinkling. "Yes, please!" she said. Then a little softer, "I have the boys this weekend. Want to come over?"

A pause and then, "Great! See you Saturday!"

I groaned and covered my head with the blanket. "Awesome," I said when she put the phone down again. "Another weekend with *Derek*. Can't wait to hear what's exciting in the lives of trees this week."

Mom didn't answer but she did stop humming, turning on the TV instead. Patrick grabbed the remote and nudged the volume up.

"Do we have to watch the news?" I asked from under the blanket.

"You don't have to watch anything at all. Mom and I are watching the news," Patrick said all snooty. He turned up the volume more.

The newscaster's voice filled the room. "Police are asking residents to be on the lookout for a German shepherd mix on the loose in the area. The owner, who says the dog is aggressive, claims teenagers taunted the dog before cutting the rope tethering it. Residents should contact the police if the dog is spotted and are warned not to approach the animal, but to call animal control. Police also ask that anyone with tips on the perpetrators should come forward."

"Wow, Kendra," a different newscaster said. "Those kids are lucky they weren't hurt."

"Yes, Steve, and we're all going to be lucky if the dog doesn't attack."

"Unreal." Mom clicked off the television. "Dinner's ready," she said.

My legs shook as I walked to the table, and I was sure Mom and Patrick would see right through me. I hadn't considered that what we were doing was illegal.

"You don't think it could've been someone you know?" Mom said to Patrick as I pulled out my seat. "I mean, the kids who messed around with that dog?"

Patrick shook his head. "No way would any of my friends be so stupid."

I gulped down pills and water, and then scooped up mashed potato. If my mouth was full the entire time, they wouldn't think to include me in on the conversation.

"The worst part is," Mom continued, "when that dog is captured, animal services will undoubtedly have to put it down."

"Put it down?" I echoed even though I was in the middle of chewing a piece of chicken.

"Disgusting," Patrick muttered.

I stuck out my chicken-coated tongue at him.

Mom sighed and said, "Put to sleep, I mean. The owner said it has a history of aggression. Now he's run off."

"But it's not the dog's fault!" I said. "It's those kids, the ones who set it free. It's their fault." Guilt barreled through me faster than that dog had and I bolted from the table. Patrick glared at me, so I added in a fake-nice voice, "Excuse me! I have to go to the bathroom. Might be a while."

Mom sighed again. "Really, Caleb? Was that necessary?"

I ignored her. When I got back, Mom was talking about the storm. "I was in the middle of a cleaning. The thunder was so loud and sudden, I jumped . . . along with the floss. Poor patient!"

"How is talking about flossing and cleaning people's mouths more appropriate than me talking about having to go to the bathroom?" I muttered, but neither Patrick nor Mom even glanced at me. I bet they had hatched a plan while I was in the bathroom. *Let's ignore Caleb.* Whatever. It wasn't going to change me. I still would do what I wanted.

"So, Caleb," Mom suddenly said, "what happened at camp when it started to storm? Where did you go?"

Not looking up from my plate, I mumbled, "We went under the pavilion."

"But the storm lasted so long. You can't have waited under the pavilion that whole time."

I pushed another forkful of mashed potato in my mouth. "We ran to the community center. No big deal."

"I bet you were soaked!" Mom said.

"It wasn't too bad," I said. "Shelly was a pain about it. She thought someone should've driven us or something. But I didn't mind."

"He was still soaked at the end of the day," Patrick added.

"Really?" Mom put down her fork. "I hope they gave you towels or something. No wonder you're wearing a sweatshirt. I bet you were freezing!"

Patrick rocked back on his seat and tilted his head. "Shelly wasn't wet at all, though."

Mom's eyes bored into the top of my head.

"A couple of the guys and I played football outside when it stopped. The grass was wet."

"Don't lie to me," Mom said, but she was smiling when I chanced looking up at her. "You jumped into the pool, didn't you?"

I grinned back. "You know me well."

Mom laughed and gathered our plates. "Well, you better take a hot bath tonight to warm up."

I handed her my glass to stack on top of the plates.

"Caleb!" she gasped. "What happened to your hand?"

Quickly I covered the long scratches with my sweatshirt sleeve. "Nothing," I said. I grasped at what to say, but this lying thing? It's sort of a skill. And I was getting good at it. Maybe too good. "The football landed in a briar bush. They don't landscape well behind the community center—you should put Derek on that—and I got a little cut up when I reached for it. No big deal."

Mom pursed her lips. "Put some antibacterial ointment on it," she said. "The last thing you need is an infection."

The whole time, even though I never glanced his way, I knew Patrick was staring at me. He hadn't stopped since he pointed out that Shelly wasn't as soaking wet as me.

-»»}-≮≮≮-

When I got to Mermaid Rock the next day, Kit wasn't there. The *World of Faerie* book was, though. A palm-size rock kept it open to the page of the blue-eyed fairy girl with the blackbird on her shoulder. A second later, Kit emerged from the woods. Part of me wanted to yell at her to be more careful with Mom's book. But it wasn't Mom's book, not anymore.

Kit added a circle of flowers to a pile of leaves at the stream's shore. "The book says the fay love flower crowns. If they approve of you, they'll accept this gift."

"Kit, the dog was on the news last night!" I said instead of responding.

"The rescue?" Kit clapped. "That's awesome. Now everyone knows she's free."

"No," I said, "they aren't calling it a rescue. They're saying we broke the law. That we were vandals and that the dog is dangerous."

Kit shook her head. "She's turned back by now, I'm sure."

"I'm talking about real life," I pressed on. "We could be in big trouble!"

"I'm talking about real life, too," she insisted. "I know I was right. She was trapped. Now she's back to who she's supposed to be."

"You don't know that," I groaned.

"Have they caught her yet?" Kit snapped. "Don't you think that's a little weird? You'd think the police would've been able to track down a giant dog by now." She leaned into me, leveling me with her storytelling face. "That's because there isn't a dog to track."

Kit climbed up onto the rock and studied the picture of the fairy with eyes like hers. Like that dog's.

I didn't want to argue about the dog or talk about her mom or anything else that made her eyes cloud over. I glared up at the boiling sun, wishing it was easier to just stick to a decision. To not always wonder if you're where you're supposed to be and doing what you should. *I do what I want.* But what do you do when you don't know what you want?

"Stop," Kit said. She shook my shoulder, scattering my thoughts. "Whatever you're thinking about, just stop." Kit slid down the rock. She lay flat on her back in the middle of the stream. It was still a bit higher than it had been thanks to the storm the night before. When she lay like that, the water trickled just past her ears, though her chin, nose, and eyes were free. She raised an arm and beckoned me down beside her.

When I didn't move right away, she raised herself up on her elbow. Her wet dark hair was black as the crow's, and it dripped down her back and into the stream. "Trust me," she said, and slapped the surface of the water beside her.

I put my phone next to the rock on the book and made my way to her. When I stood beside her, my shadow covered her face. "This is stupid," I said. "No one lies in the middle of a stream."

But the water clogged Kit's ears and she didn't answer, just smiled so wide the corners of her mouth dipped into the water. She reached up and tugged on my hand. I lowered into the water. It was cool but not freezing, especially since the air was so hot that day. I lay on my back, letting the water pour all around me from the top of my head, over my ears, and through the hand still clasped by Kit.

I couldn't hear anything but the water. Couldn't feel anything but the pull of its current and the blanket of air over us. Couldn't see anything but the patch of startling blue sky over my face. Couldn't even think of anything but this one perfect moment and the girl sharing it with me.

And I knew I was exactly where I was supposed to be.

Hours passed before I thought to look for the flower crown. But the shoreline was empty.

━━➤➤➤ ⫷⫷⫷━━

I meant to go to camp at least one day that week, but I never did. I didn't the week after, either.

One Friday, Kit and I spent the day lying on our stomachs in the grass outside her house, reading *The World of Faerie*, the book spread out between us, while we shared my lunch.

I was too tired for much more than that. I guessed I hadn't slept all that well the past few nights. I kept having nightmares about wild dogs with blue eyes, police officers knocking on my door, shattering glass, and the thing that happened (the one I was never going to talk about ever) in the barn before we left.

I actually fell asleep, my face on the edge of the book. It was one of those terrible where-am-I wake ups, complete with a thick line of drool running from my cheek to the page. Quickly I pulled my phone out of my pocket to check the time. Phew! It was only a little after one o'clock. "Kit?" I called out, and then doubled over coughing. Sleeping on my stomach did that sometimes.

Her laughter reached my ears before I spotted her sitting under a nearby evergreen tree with her legs outstretched like two sides of a triangle. Something small and dark hopped between them. I must've really been out of it because when I stood, I was dizzy for a minute. For a stupid second I even thought Kit *was* a fairy.

But then the world straightened up and I saw it was just Kit, and the small dark thing hopping between her outstretched legs was a crow. It must've been a baby or at least really young because it didn't seem all that interested in flying. It just hopped forward and back, its mouth wide as it croaked out a *cah, cah*.

The bird was covered in fluffy black feathers and had huge

bluish-gray eyes. I swear, the bird's eyes were blue. What were the chances that Kit, the dog, and now this bird would all have the same blue eyes? "Do you see?" Kit asked as she tossed it a bit of sandwich crust left over from our lunch and it wobbled forward, its mouth outstretched like a red kite in the middle of its face as it swooped and gobbled up the bread.

"What's going on?" I whispered.

Kit held out her finger, and the bird hopped onto it and then up her arm. He was about the size of my whole hand and so fluffy he looked perfectly round. Now that the bread was down his belly, his red kite mouth hung open again. "I heard this noise when you fell asleep." She laughed as the bird croaked again because it was like he was helping her tell the story. Maybe he was. "And when I went to explore, here he was."

Kit lifted her arm so the bird was level with her nose. "It's just like the book, Caleb," she said, her voice low and her eyes round with stories. "I think his name should be Puck."

"Puck?" I glanced around the trees hanging over us. "Where are his parents?"

Kit grinned. "I don't know. He's here by himself!"

I squinted at a basketball-size bundle of twigs super high up in the pine tree. "I think that's his nest. Maybe he fell out. I bet the parents will look for him."

A flash of black darted across the sky. "*Cah, cah!*" screeched a crow overhead. The little bird fluffed his wings.

Kit shook her head. "He's supposed to be with me."

"We can go into town, maybe to the library, and figure out what to do, how to get him help." I thought of the dog, with its bright blue eyes. Was she okay now?

Kit bent her legs and stood. "No," she said. "He's mine." She smiled at me and added, "The fairies saw that I'm learning more about them. They've given me a gift."

"I don't know, Kit," I said as she walked toward the house. "Do you know how to take care of a baby like that? Can you take care of it?"

"You better go, Caleb," she said without turning. "I think my mom is coming home soon."

➤➤➤ ⫷⫷⫷

I didn't bother to backtrack to the park. My legs were extra heavy as I trudged across the stream toward my house. I really wanted to take another nap, this time in my bed. Besides, I knew I didn't have to watch out for the bus. Patrick had borrowed the car so he could coordinate this fund-raising thing with Dr. Edwards' office; Mom had told me to just use the key under the mat and let myself in after camp, that Patrick wouldn't be home until after four o'clock.

I did look around to make sure the coast was clear before leaving the woods, though. Here's the creepy thing. I was more worried about what was *in* the woods than I was of anyone catching me *leaving* the woods. Ever since Kit had gone inside, I had felt like someone was watching me. It was probably just my imagination.

The crow I had spotted earlier seemed to be traveling with me across the woods, always swooping a few dozen feet above my head. And the woods around me rustled, once so suddenly and close I screamed, sure the dog was about to come back for my entire hand instead of just a scrape or two. But it was a fat chipmunk, squeaking as it burst from behind a tree, closely followed by a second.

I tried to shake the feeling, but it was good to be inside my house. I just wished I hadn't spotted the crow settling in a tree in my front yard, watching as I closed and locked the front door.

CHAPTER TWELVE

Here is something I've never told anyone: One time, when Brad and I were little, like in third grade, we told our moms we were going to ride our bikes around the block a couple times. But in reality? We rode all the way to the school and back. It was the middle of summer and we thought it'd be cool to run around the playground when it was totally empty. Only when we got there, the playground was full of toddlers and preschoolers. There must've been a mommy meeting or something. Plus, as soon as we arrived, we both sort of realized how angry our parents were going to be about us being so far from home. So we returned, only Brad suggested a shortcut across the field. And that meant getting to the road by going around the back of this old boarded-up church where older kids hung out.

I didn't know any of them and neither did Brad, but he said hi anyway as we passed, walking our bikes since my legs were feeling a little wobbly. All of the older kids ignored us. All of them except this one guy—he must've been about fourteen. "Hey," he said. He smiled, but it was the type of smile that is only lips and teeth, you know? The kind someone might plaster on for a photo. He curled his hand, beckoning us to the side of the church where a lilac tree bloomed, stretching up and over the boarded-up steps.

"Let's go," I muttered to Brad.

But Brad was already rolling his bike toward the guy. What was I supposed to do? I followed him.

"Want to see something cool?" the guy asked, and he parted some of the branches of the lilac bush. From a tree behind us, a small bird screeched and I jumped at the sudden sound. The guy rolled his eyes. "Look," he said. There between the branches was a little nest.

"Wow," Brad whispered, and he leaned forward on tiptoe to see it. He glanced back at me and smiled. A real smile, with eyes, too. I crowded over his shoulder to see. In the middle of the nest was a little pinkish-blue egg. Next to it was a just-hatched bird. It was the ugliest thing I had ever seen—it looked like someone took a wad of chewed-up bubblegum and rolled it in a dust bunny. The bird's eyes were the size of pencil erasers and sealed shut. Its beak opened and closed soundlessly and its too-big legs curled under its body. The halves of its broken shell lay beside it.

"Wow," I echoed. I couldn't look at it for more than a couple seconds, but couldn't look away for long, either. It was hideously beautiful. I know this sounds strange, but it made my knees hurt, like just looking at the helpless bird hollowed them a little.

The older guy leaned over both of us. He scooped up the bird in his hand. The bird in the tree screeched again. He thrust the baby toward us so it was just a couple inches from our faces. I couldn't help it—I coughed and it turned into a cry. Brad, he reached back and squeezed my wrist. "Stop," he whispered, and I didn't know if he was talking to me or the older boy, who still had his lips pulled back from his teeth in a not-smile.

The older boy dropped the baby bird onto the sidewalk. "Stupid babies," he muttered with a not-laugh.

Brad grabbed my elbow, pulling me back toward our bikes and away from the older kids. But first I scooped up the baby bird—it was light as a used tea bag in my hand—and placed it back in the nest. It was the bravest thing I've ever done. As we walked away, the mother bird flew to the nest, settling on top of and quieting the baby.

I hadn't thought about that for a long time. I guessed seeing the baby crow with Kit today made me think of it. Inside my house, I sank onto the couch and closed my eyes. As I fell asleep again, I heard that whispery plop of the baby bird hitting the sidewalk.

-»»».«««-

"Hey, wake up." Patrick loomed over me, holding the throw pillow he had just whapped against my shoulder.

185

"What?" I groaned. He hit me again when I rolled onto my other side.

"Get up," he said. "Your friend's here."

"What!" I jolted upright, then wobbled a little as my body adjusted to being on its feet again.

Patrick steadied me by grabbing my shoulders. "You okay?"

"I'm fine," I said, shrugging off his grip and heading to the door. What was Kit doing here? I gulped down panic. Did it have something to do with the dog? Were the police onto us?

I half ran to the front door, stopping with a halt when I saw who stood there: Brad, twirling a football in his hand. "Hey," Brad said, and threw the ball at me.

I caught it automatically, pulling it to my side. "Hey."

"Wanna go outside, toss it around a little?"

"Uh . . ." I looked around, as if some reason for why I couldn't might materialize. "I told Mom I'd clean up my room."

"Oh, can we just—" Brad said at the same time Patrick butt in, "Mom's not going to check. Derek's giving her a lift home and staying for dinner. She's going to be busy."

"Fine, let's go." I shoved the ball into Brad's chest as I passed him to head outside. Brad followed, but super slowly, pulling shut the screen door.

I backed up a few yards and held out my hands for Brad to toss the football. He did, but weakly so it just sort of flung toward me and landed with a thud near my feet. "What's up?" I asked.

Brad shoved his hands in his pockets as I scooped up the ball, so I didn't bother to throw it back to him. "Where've you been, man? I haven't seen you around in forever."

I shrugged. "You must've missed me. I've been around." I mimed throwing the ball back to him, and he held up his hands again. The ball landed with a soft thump against his palms.

This time, he tossed it back with more force so I had to jump a foot to catch it. "I thought I'd see you at the pool—all the other camp kids are there. You're not. Shelly says you've got other things going on."

I threw the ball again, buying time to consider my words. Who knew Shelly would have my back like that? "Yeah, just dealing with some stuff, I guess."

"Is it—are you . . ." Brad twisted the ball around in his hands. "Are you okay, Caleb? I thought maybe you were sick or something."

I held up my hands for him to throw the ball back. "No, I've been all right."

Brad held on to the ball, rolling it in his hands and staring down at it. "Are we all right?" he said. He looked up at me and I felt my mouth go dry. "Did I do something, make you mad or something?"

My teeth clenched together. Did he do something? Not really. And yet, he had. I took a deep breath. *You throw a shadow over me. All the time. I'm never beside you. I'm always behind you. And now you're freaking out because you don't have me there, always ready to make you shine just by comparison. "Look at him," everyone thinks, "isn't he awesome to be best buds with the sick kid when he could be friends with anyone?"*

But that's not what I really said. Instead, I blurted out, "No, man. Of course not." This time when I held up my hands, he threw the ball back to me. We tossed it back and forth for a couple minutes, Brad having to jump and dive for my tosses while his always went straight to my open hands. Brad went on and on about the football team, how they won their first scrimmage and how he was named captain of the twelve-and-under league ("Of course you were," I said and he grinned), and how all the guys play volleyball in the pool after practice.

"You should be there, Caleb," he said. And for a second, I sort of believed him.

"Do you ever think about the baby bird?" I asked right in the middle of Brad telling me about some awesome play the team figured out at practice the day before.

Brad caught the ball and turned to a statue for a second. After a long pause, he said, "No." We didn't talk for a long time after that, just threw the ball back and forth until Derek pulled into the driveway with Mom.

"Brad!" Mom called, her lip glossy smile shining. "Would you like to stay for dinner?"

"No, thank you. I should be getting home." Brad's eyebrows peaked as he looked back at me, and I knew he was wondering who Derek was and what he was doing with Mom. I sort of shrugged.

"Thanks for stopping by," I said.

"Maybe I'll see you tomorrow," he said, "at the pool."

Mom and Derek disappeared into the house, talking the whole time.

"Maybe," I said back.

⇢⇥⇤⇠

Mom's laughter poured through the house. Strange how odd it sounded to hear her laugh. I guess I hadn't really heard it in a while. It made the house feel different. Like I was a visitor. I went into the kitchen to grab a juice box and a bag of chips to hold me over until dinner. Derek was telling Mom something about a picky client who kept nailing him with all of these ridiculous requests, and Mom was cracking up, her face shining. Both of them smiled at me when I walked into the room to grab the juice from the fridge, but I felt strange suddenly. I didn't know if I should sit next to Mom in the kitchen or be in the living room, where I'd overhear her and Derek's conversation. My room seemed like the safest place, except that when I made my way down the hall, there was Patrick leaning against the wall on the other side of my door.

"What was all that about?" he asked.

"Oh," I said and slurped on the juice box. I swear, they only fill those things with three sips of fruit punch. "Derek's telling her about some guy wanting a tree shaped like a poodle in his front yard." I shrugged.

189

"No, not that." Patrick lowered his head so he was staring me down. "I meant Brad. What did he mean by not seeing you in a while? You'd think he'd see you all the time. You know, since you spend all day at camp."

I shrugged again, taking a useless pull on the juice box straw just because I knew the sound annoyed him. "Guess we keep missing each other."

"But you're at camp all day, right?"

"Where else would I be?" I ducked around him and into my room.

"Right." Patrick headed down the hall just as Mom's laughter rippled again. He paused and then doubled back to his room, too.

-»»».««««-

We ate out on the patio again that night. I wondered if Derek got sick of being outside all the time, but he smiled nonstop, so I guessed not.

I filled my tacos with extra cheese, sour cream, guacamole, and beans. Mom gave me a look so I added some lettuce, too. Mom even made dessert . . . sort of. She brought out marshmallows, graham crackers, and chocolate for us to make s'mores over the grill. But we never got around to actually turning on the grill. Instead, we just ate the ingredients all separate or smooshed together cold. Patrick talked forever about the fund-raiser—they were going to have a 5K race to raise CF awareness in a month, and he had spent the day going from business to business requesting donations. "I scored more funds than any other volunteer by double," he finished as Mom clapped and Derek fist bumped him. I didn't say anything. Wonder how many of those donations were because Patrick told everyone his kid brother had the crap luck to be born with a fatal disease?

"Check this out," Derek said suddenly. He tore off a tiny bit of a marshmallow and then strode out to the middle of the deck. The sun was set but the sky was still holding on to color at the tree line. It kind of looked like a dark rainbow filling up the whole sky—a curve of gold, then reddish yellow, then blue, then indigo, then almost-black. A couple birds glided overhead, even though I didn't think birds really flew all that much at night.

Derek paused a moment and then threw the bit of marshmallow straight up into the sky. One of the birds swooped suddenly and caught the sugary treat before it even began to fall back down.

"Wow. What just happened?" I asked.

"A bat." Derek grinned and threw another piece into the air for another bat.

Mom shuddered. "I didn't realize we had bats."

"Be glad you do," Derek said. "That citronella candle you lit can only do so much. Bats are the best for getting rid of mosquitoes."

"How did it see that tiny piece of marshmallow?" I asked. "I thought they were blind."

Derek smiled again as he squinted up at the darkening sky. "They use echolocation. The bat didn't know it was a marshmallow—I'm sure that was just a bonus. Obviously not part of its diet, but a little piece like that won't hurt him."

"But how—"

Derek smiled. "It only knew something was flying through the air, so it zeroed in and *boom*. Caught it. Pretty fascinating."

I nodded but didn't say anything else. Derek, I could tell, really got into this nature stuff. He seemed to be one of those people who just holds on to information, storing little details like archived files of a website.

"Tell the boys of the birds you were talking about yesterday," Mom said when it got too quiet again. She motioned for Patrick to sit back down when he rose to gather up the plates. "This is so cool, Patrick."

"Oh," Derek said, and pulled out his chair from the table a little to rock back. "This family of crows lives at a property I help manage. The fledglings are just beginning to leave the nest."

I sat up a little in my seat. "Fledglings?"

"Yeah," Derek said. "The babies. Crows are pretty amazing. They live as families like us in a lot of ways. The parents take care of the babies, but the older siblings help out, too, bringing the babies food and watching over them. They have whole communities, actually, with everyone pitching in."

Mom rested her elbows on the table, placing her chin on her hands. "Tell them about the babies!" she cooed.

Derek chuckled. "So, yeah, these fledglings—practically little balls of black fluff—fall from their nests, right? But they can't fly yet to get back up there. So the older siblings keep an eye on them, hopping along behind them, bringing them food. But, I guess just like our families, older brothers and sisters get sick of the newbies after a while. This one guy I work with, Hank, he sees a baby all by itself and thinks it's hurt or something. So he picks it up. Big mistake."

"Why?" I asked, my heart pounding up in my throat.

"Because he ticked off the entire crow community. At first everything was cool, he was just talking to the baby, right? But then he went and took the baby with him into the truck. Nice guy, he was going to take it to a friend of his who works at an animal sanctuary. But the crows didn't know that—they just figured he was stealing the baby."

Derek took a pull from the beer Mom handed him. "His friend tells him, 'Hey, fledglings hang out at the base of trees. It's cool, he's not abandoned.' And he warns Hank to bring the baby back to the tree as soon as possible. So Hank heads right back. Immediately, a crow flies over him and Hank gets this giant dropping right on the middle of his truck's windshield. When he steps out, the baby still inside the truck, to wipe the mess off, another one swoops over him— low enough to make this giant bear of a man scream and cower. Then another one swoops, again and again, over him."

"You'd think he'd have gotten the message," Patrick quipped.

"Oh, he did!" Derek laughed again. "Hank took the baby out of the truck. Put it back where he had found it. He even tossed a bit of his sandwich at the baby and backed off with his hands up." Derek took another drink and shook his head. "But it was too late."

"What do you mean?" I asked.

"The birds had marked him as a bad job. Every time he got to work, they'd gather in the trees and screech at him. They took turns dive-bombing him as he mowed the grass. Every single day, his truck—but no one else's around him—would be covered in droppings. Poor guy had to swap out with someone else and work at properties miles from his house.

"Here's the weirdest thing: that was two years ago. Just last week, the regular guy on that property was sick and the client couldn't wait—needed lawn care right away because they were having a wedding. Enough time passed where that fledgling should've been grown, right? Hank didn't want to go, but I talked him into it."

"What happened?" I asked again as Derek finished the beer.

"The birds remembered him. Same thing—dive-bombing his head, using his truck as target practice." Derek leaned forward so I could see his serious face in the darkened sky. "Strangest thing. But I did a little research, and it's true. Crows remember—and they don't like to be messed with."

My leg drummed under the table.

"The baby, though, he sure was cute. Bright blue eyes, fluffy little guy." Derek stood and helped Mom and Patrick pick up plates.

"Wait!" I said. "Blue eyes? I thought crows had dark eyes."

"All babies have blue eyes when they're hatched," Derek said. "They get darker later."

I stood, pushing out the chair behind me. "I've got to go," I said.

"Where?" Mom asked.

"To bed," I lied. "I . . . I've got to go to bed."

"Are you feeling okay?" Mom asked.

"Yeah, I'm fine. Just tired. I'll do my physio and get to sleep, okay?"

Derek looked from me to Mom and back. "I'll head home, okay, Steph? Thanks for dinner."

"No," Mom said. "No, we were going to watch that show, remember?"

"Yeah," I said, "stay. I'm just going to go to bed. That's all." I kissed Mom's cheek. "Thanks for dinner."

"Good night, love," Mom said.

Patrick raised an eyebrow at me as I passed him on the way to my bedroom, but he didn't say anything.

I went to my room and locked the door. I set the vest machine so the noise would carry out into the room and then eased open my bedroom window.

I had to tell Kit the truth and it couldn't wait until Monday. It couldn't wait another minute. I had to tell her all baby crows have blue eyes.

CHAPTER THIRTEEN

The sky was light enough for me to see the bats swooping above me as I darted across the yard to the woods. But inside the tree line, the dark was thick as a blanket over my eyes. I turned on the flashlight app on my phone and held it in front of me; the little circle of light made what was just outside of it somehow scarier. I didn't realize I was at the stream until my sneakers soaked up water to my toes. I kicked off my shoes and ran across the rocks. Of course, I stepped wrong and slipped in the stream in the middle, landing with a thud on my butt since I was too worried about holding my phone up and out of the water to brace my fall. I jumped back up and kept going, phone held out to light the narrow path our feet had forged over the past few weeks to Kit's house.

A bird called out as I ran, making me jump. All around me, the woods rustled. I even thought I heard a howl, but it was probably an owl or something. My mind filled up the blackness around me with a million images that fluttered faster than wings—dark fairies with faces folded like tree bark, winged girls morphing into giant dogs, crows with sharpened beaks, police officers crouching behind trees. None of them made sense, but I ran from them as much as I hurried toward Kit. I had to tell her she was wrong, that the baby crow wasn't a gift but something she had stolen. I had to tell her it wasn't magic that gave the bird blue eyes, that it was just the way it was born.

It wasn't until I reached the edge of the woods and was halfway across Kit's sparse and dirt-packed lawn that I realized I might get her in trouble by barging into her house this late.

But judging from the loud music pumping out of the open windows, no one was sleeping. Kit's mom's car was parked by the house and most of the windows were dimly lit with lamps, including the turret high above. I shoved my phone in my pocket and picked up a quarter-size pebble by my feet. *I can do this*, I thought as I reared back. But instead of hitting Kit's window like I had hoped, the rock slammed against the side of the house. I crouched, ready to run if someone stormed out of the house to catch me, but nothing happened.

"What are you doing here?" a small voice hissed instead. *Kit.* I breathed out and hurried to the porch. I almost didn't see her. Kit, she usually sits right in the middle of things, soaking up the sun on Mermaid Rock or sprawled across a patch of grass. This Kit was folded up in the corner of the porch farthest away from the front door. Her face, pale and round in the weak light, was crossed by porch rail shadows. "You have to leave," she whispered before I could speak.

"I have to tell you," I said, my words coming out in bursts as I tried to muffle the cough boiling up my throat. "It's about the bird."

The floorboards inside the house creaked. A shadow person moved by the windows. Kit's head whipped toward the house and back to me. "You have to go. You have to go *right now*."

"Are you okay?" I whispered back. I grabbed the porch rails, my hands curling against them. "Is everything all right?"

"Just *go*," she whispered back. She scrunched shut her eyes.

"Kit!" stormed the shadow person inside the house. "Kit! Where the heck are you? Off crying still about that stupid bird." Through the window, I spotted Kit's mom throwing up her arms. I crouched below the porch just as she threw open the door, a shaft of light from inside making an orange triangle across the front stoop onto the ground.

I tried to be invisible, crouched there in the dark, but my stupid body wanted to move in a thousand directions at once. I shook all over, willing myself to be silent and still, not that my body ever listened to anything I told it to do. A huffing cough erupted out of me just as Kit's hand darted between the rails and shoved my head lower to the ground.

"There you are," said the shadow person, her voice cold. Something clicked and then I heard a steady pull in of breath. A moment later, I smelled tobacco smoke. "Hiding in the corner like a stupid dog."

Kit pushed further into the corner. I covered both my hands across my mouth.

"Get over here, Kit."

"I don't want to," Kit whispered.

"Come here?" This time the words were a question, soft and gentler. The woman stumbled a little, and Kit rushed forward, half crawling until she was by her mother's side. I peeked up over the porch without really thinking.

Kit's mother was a taller, skinnier, harder version of Kit. Like if Kit was an unfolded new leaf, her mom was the brittle-edged late-summer version. Kit flinched as her mom's arm lurched out. I shuddered, remembering the bruise that had only just faded from Kit's face. The one she got from falling down the tree. Unless she hadn't fallen.

"Come here," her mother said. Her words slurred like she was speaking in cursive. "What do we know about raising birds?"

Kit didn't say anything, but tucked her body under her mom's, holding her up.

"Had to put it out there. Bird's gotta toughen up. It's nature's way." The cigarette tip was a red laser point at her mother's mouth.

"Can I just put it back?" Kit whispered. "Back to the tree where we—I mean *I*—got it?"

"You're lucky I didn't put the thing out of its misery," Kit's shadow mom snapped. "Still could." She lurched backward, but Kit wrapped her arm around her waist.

"No, please, Mama!" Kit hiccupped.

Her mom paused and moved back toward the door. "I'm going back to the doctor tomorrow, Kit-Kat," she said. "Gonna go tomorrow and get back on the meds. Gonna get better."

"I know," Kit murmured. "I know."

Kit opened the door with one hand, so again the light spread out from it like a spotlight. Her shadow mom cried. I could tell by the quick, shattering peak and fall of her narrow shoulders. "Grandmom knew how to take care of us both. I don't know how."

"I know," Kit said again, and dragged her mom forward toward the door.

"I'll go to the doctor tomorrow. Take the medicine. I won't hurt you again, Kit-Kat. Not ever again." They took another step, this time through the doorway. "What do we know 'bout raising birds?" she slurred again.

The door closed so just a sliver of light escaped from it across the porch and onto a patch of lawn. There was a small black ball of feathers. Somehow I had passed right by it before without seeing it.

For a horrible second I thought the bird had died. It was so still.

Then its tiny wings rustled. A soft peep rumbled from it. Though my whole body still shook from seeing Kit's shadow mom, I crawled forward. As I cupped my hands around the bird, I nearly felt the scrape of a half dozen talons and beak into my back, so much sharper than that of the dog. But it was just my mind creating more images in the dark. I picked up the baby and carried it back to the tree, waiting until I was a few feet from the house to shift the bird into one hand and fish out my phone with the other to light the way. At the base of the tree where Kit had found it earlier, I put down the bird.

"It's okay," I whispered to it, because it hopped toward me again as I stood to leave. "Your family is here." This time I knew I wasn't imagining the rustle of wings I heard in the tree above me. "I'm sorry," I whispered to them, too. "I'm sorry."

-》》》.《《《-

I bolted down the narrow trail to the stream. This time I didn't fall as I rushed across the ankle-deep water. At the other side, I sprinted toward my house. How much time had passed? A glance at the time on my phone told me it was less than ten minutes. Could that be true?

Outside my bedroom, I realized pulling myself into a window was going to be much harder than crawling out. I tried to lift myself up to the window's ledge but I never could do a pull-up. I scrambled, my feet hitting the house as I tried to find traction to kick up and over the stupid ledge. Just when I slipped backward, an arm darted out, the hand wrapping just behind my elbow and yanking me into my bedroom, where I fell with a thud onto the carpet.

I jumped to my feet to see Derek standing in front of me. Derek flashed a quick grim smile and his eyes dropped down to my bare, wet feet. Then he stepped aside and I saw Mom standing in the doorway, the bobby pin she had used to pop open the door in her hand.

"Where in the world have you been, Caleb?" Mom yelled. Her face was scary red except for her tight white lips. "The vest machine ran for more than ten straight minutes without you stopping to cough. I knocked on the door—no answer. Turned the handle on a locked door. Caleb!" She rushed forward, grabbing me by fistfuls of T-shirt. Her eyes were wet and huge. "Do you know what I thought? Do you have any idea what I thought happened in here, to you alone while I'm out there *laughing*?" Mom shook so hard her hands ricocheted off my collarbone like a heartbeat. She crushed me against her, releasing her grip on my shirt and pulling me against her, tears scalding my neck. "Don't you leave like that, Caleb. Don't you ever leave like that!"

"I'm sorry," I mumbled.

Mom dropped her arms just as quickly as she had grabbed hold of me. Now she pushed me back to stare at my face. "Where were you? What were you doing? What were you *thinking*?"

My throat dried up. I couldn't make a single sound, not a single explanation could come to the surface.

Behind me, Derek shuffled. "I'm—I'm going to head out. 'Night, Steph. Caleb." I didn't look away from Mom and she didn't glance over at Derek as he stepped around us to the door. "'Night, Patrick," he said as he passed my brother lurking just outside the door.

"Answer me, Caleb!" Mom kind of shook my shoulders. "Where were you?"

I stared down at my dirty toes.

"He was outside," Patrick said from the hallway. "I saw him crawling out of his window from my bedroom."

I glared over at my perfect brother. But my death stare had nothing on Mom's. "You saw him," she repeated, "but you didn't say anything to me? *Patrick!*"

Patrick didn't look at me or Mom. "You're making too big a deal out of it, Mom. He was just out there, throwing marshmallow pieces to bats."

I gulped, fighting to keep my face smooth. Did my brother just cover for me? My voice shook with the lie when I said, "I wanted to try feeding them, but I didn't want you guys to make fun of me."

Mom stared hard at my face for a full minute. I tried not to squirm. At last, she let go of my shoulders. "You can't lie to me, Caleb. We don't do that. We don't lie to each other in this house." *Anymore.* I could read the words she left unsaid in the thick air between us. *Not since Dad left.*

Mom got to her feet, smoothed her hands along her pants, and sighed. "Now, if you'll excuse me, I need to call Derek and apologize for my son's rudeness. It's becoming a bit of a habit, actually. One that stops *today*."

I stopped Patrick as he walked back to his room. "Why'd you cover for me?" I asked.

Patrick stared at me, his eyes narrowed. "I didn't actually see you leave. I would've told on you if I had. I'm not sure why I'm covering for you now, to tell you the truth. But don't make me regret it." He crossed his arms. "Whatever's going on—whatever you're lying about or hiding—you better stop. It's not just the lying, either. You skipped out on a treatment."

He glanced over to where Mom and I had been a moment earlier. Maybe he felt some of the slap from her stinging words, too.

—⟫⟩⟩⟨⟨⟨—

Saturday morning, Mom woke me way too early. It had taken me forever to fall asleep—my mind was full of winged girls morphing into wolves, birds with sharpened talons and beaks, stream water pouring over my nose. "Come on, Caleb," she said, her voice brisk as the shake she gave my shoulder. "Wake up."

I groaned into my pillow. "Why?" I yelled, even as I sat up and shrugged on the vest. I clicked on the movie, picking back up where Captain America watches Bucky fall from the train.

Mom checked the machine and tossed a tissue box next to

204

me. "As soon as you're done, I want you in the living room. Do you understand?"

"Why?" I grumbled through the nebulizer mask. "Can't I just go back to sleep?"

"No," Mom said. She stepped toward the door, started to close it, then seemed to change her mind. She opened it wider instead. "We're having a family meeting."

"What?" I moaned.

At the same time, I heard another, deeper voice drift down the hall from the kitchen. "Where the heck is the sugar?" Awesome. Dad was here, too.

I stretched out the vest treatment as long as I could, huffing for a full five minutes after the machine ran for five, then doing it again. I went an extra five after that, too. When I knew I couldn't put it off any longer, I brushed my teeth and ventured down the hall to where Mom and Dad waited. Both sat in armchairs on either side of the couch. When Dad left, he took the chairs we had. These were new ones, covered in flowers and stiff material. Mom looked like she perched on the edge of a throne. Dad just looked uncomfortable and annoyed.

"Your father and I have been discussing some recent issues we've had with you," Mom began the moment I sat down on the couch between them. "We've seen a tremendous shift in your attitude and behavior since school let out this year."

My head pounded. I let it fall back to the top of the couch as Mom continued. "You're short-tempered and rude, mean to your brother, and I heard that you were unkind to Kristie."

"Unkind?" Dad snorted. "He hacked in her face. She threw up for an hour afterward!"

I glanced at Mom, whose mouth was awfully twitchy. She looked away and when she turned back, her face was stern again. "Right, and that stunt you pulled last night—sneaking out of your window—we can't let this continue." She took a deep breath. "Is there something you'd like to talk about? There have been a lot of . . . changes recently." She glanced at Dad.

I rolled my eyes. Of course they'd want to blame Kristie's baby or Derek, to make it about them. "Believe it or not, Mom, I do what *I* want."

Mom's eyes narrowed. "This. This right here. This is the attitude to which I'm referring."

"Pull yourself together, kid," Dad said, and he leaned forward so his elbows were on his knees. "Life's not going to go the way you want, but you can't go around making everyone else miserable!"

This time I was the one who snorted.

"What?" Dad barked.

"*Life isn't going to go the way I want?* Really. That's one way to put CF."

Dad threw his arms up, waving them out like he was fanning away smoke. "I can't handle the drama with this one."

Mom's lips twisted. "Caleb, I feel"—she cleared her throat—"*we* feel something must've happened to trigger this."

"But it's time to grow up!" Dad crossed his arms.

"That would be nice," I snapped without thinking. Mom reared back as if shoved.

"Caleb!" she gasped while Dad groaned. "Caleb, do you need someone to talk with? Between the divorce, the new"—she swallowed as if the next word was a piece of taffy lodged in her throat—"baby, we understand you might need help sorting your feelings."

Dad rolled his eyes. "What he needs is to toughen up. Deal with what's around him and stop making everyone else cater to *him*."

Mom scooted to the edge of her chair, making me focus on her instead of him. "We can discuss having you see a therapist if you think that'd help, honey."

"Sure, my health insurance isn't saddled enough," Dad muttered. He, too, scooted forward. "Caleb, listen to me. You're old enough to understand that you are not the center of the universe. Man up. Your brother never had any trouble being a decent human being. Time for you to do the same."

Mom crossed her arms. "What your father is *trying* to say, I think, is that we love you. We're worried about you. But we can't allow you to continue being unkind and deceitful. Things like sneaking outside. Like mouthing off. Like lying. These things have to *stop*. How can we help you?"

"Steph, *we* don't need to help him. *He* needs to do it."

"George," Mom said, mimicking Dad's tone, "he is a *child*. It's *our* job to help him."

"And he's always going to be a child if he never has to do anything on his own." Dad's face flushed. He lounged back on the stiff chair. If a mic had been in his hand, I was sure he would've dropped it.

"Yes, he's always going to be *my* child, and I'll parent him as I see fit." Mom stood. "You may leave now. I'm sure Kristie is in need of some of your stellar parenting insight." Mic drop, Mom.

But Dad didn't go, of course—too busy trying to come up with a better one-liner. This could go on for hours. I slunk down the hall and fell back asleep before they realized I had left.

-»»>·««-

Okay. Here's the truth.

I never saved the first baby bird.

I left it on the sidewalk.

CHAPTER FOURTEEN

Sunday morning, Mom woke me up early. Again.

"Why?" I bellowed into my pillow. "Why?"

"We're going to church," she said. I opened my eyes at that. My family, we're not church-going people. Mom prayed a lot—Hail, Marys mostly, and usually when she's driving on four-lane highways or through snowstorms—and I have pictures from my baptism, but other than that, we just didn't go to church much.

"Why?" I asked again, this time sitting up in the bed.

Mom pushed clothes around in my closet. "Do you have any pants with a zipper?" she asked.

"No," I replied. I tended to go for elastic waist. "Comfort trumps fashion any day of the week."

"Not on Sundays. Not at church," Mom replied. "I'll find

something of Patrick's for you to borrow."

"Awesome." I snapped my vest into place.

A half hour later, I shoveled scrambled eggs into my mouth with a paper towel shoved around my too-loose collared shirt and baggy khakis. Patrick's clothes, even the ones from when he was my age, were enormous. "I look like a little kid playing dress-up," I muttered around the eggs while Mom told me to hurry, hurry, hurry.

"We're going to be late!"

"Then let's not go." I unbuttoned the first button on the shirt.

"We're going." Mom took the plate from me and handed me a banana. "You can eat this in the car."

"Let me grab my sneakers." I groaned. And then I remembered: My sneakers! I was so stupid! My sneakers were still by the stream. I had spent all day Saturday lying around, never putting on shoes or even looking for them. But I had left my shoes—the only shoes that fit me—on the shore of the stream when I had run away to Kit's house on Friday night!

"You are not wearing sneakers to church." Mom crossed her arms.

"Okay," I said. Her mouth popped open. She closed it. It popped open again.

"Okay," she said back.

"Does Patrick have an old pair of shoes I can borrow, too? My sneakers are the only shoes that fit."

210

Mom nodded. Two minutes later, she was shoving newspaper into the toes of Patrick's old oxfords, ones he had to wear for his orchestra concerts, and my clown costume was complete. I put on the shoes without pointing out that they slipped off my ankles every time I took a step despite the newspaper. "Glad to see our discussion yesterday has had an impact," Mom said when we loaded into the car.

I didn't answer.

➺⟫⟫⟪⟪⟪⟪⟵

We didn't talk too much after church. Derek was there; it was his church, apparently. I tried not to let that annoy me too much. I stood next to him in the pew, taking cues from him on when to sit and stand. At one point, we even had to kneel with our hands clasped in front of us. It was like I was acting out a role in a skit. I played the part of a contrite kid learning to pray.

Derek leaned toward me and whispered, "My mom used to tell me angels danced on the tips of my fingers when I held them like that."

"That's kind of creepy," I said without thinking.

Derek laughed into his clasped hands, his big shoulders quaking with the silent chuckles. "That's what I always thought, too." He lowered his voice further when the person in front of us turned around with raised eyebrows. "I used to sit so stiff, not wanting an angel to trip and fall because I couldn't be still. Wasn't until I was a teenager that I figured out that had been Ma's intent all along."

211

"She told you that so you'd sit still?" I whispered back.

Derek nodded, his eyes still laughing at the corners. "Worked, too. Most stories we tell kids, it's just because we want them to do something. Not wander off in the woods, never take the easy way out, don't trust strangers."

"Sit still in church," I added.

Derek nodded. "She might've believed it, though. I was pretty bummed when I figured it out. Still hope it's true." He bumped into my shoulder, making my knee slip off the cushion and my hands dip. "There goes Gabriel!"

I snorted into my hands, both of us cracking up harder when Mom turned her death glare on us.

Even though most of the time I was just going through the motions, the actual being there in church was kind of nice, I guessed. I didn't point out to Mom that we were, by far, the nicest dressed people there. Most of them, including Derek, wore jeans and T-shirts. The minister, a tall white-haired woman with huge chunky earrings and a soft voice, put her hand over her heart during her sermon. She read a bit by some guy named John and then spoke a lot about peace, about how the path to it is following the quiet voice inside. "This voice will guide you, shake you from the inside out when it knows you're ignoring it. Follow it, follow this divine instrument, and you will find peace."

It sounded nice and all, but what if that voice was telling you to do something different all the time? What if you had a couple voices, all lobbying for their own path? A narrow one through the woods or a sidewalk to the park. What did you do then?

I do what I want.

Near the end of the service, you were supposed to shake hands with the people around you and say, "Peace be with you." But this church was small, so everyone shook hands with everyone. "Peace be with you." "Peace be with you." My mind twisted it a couple times into "Piece be with you" and I imagined each person getting a piece of something pressed into their palms. Maybe a piece of a cookie or something. "Piece be with you."

Maybe a piece of something else, though, too.

⤙⟫⟫⟩ ⟨⟨⟨⤚

I had wanted to go to camp on Monday. Just because it was time, you know? I had to make appearances or this whole gig was up, right? Not because I didn't want to see Kit. Not because of the crows. Not because of the baby bird or the wild dog or the blue eyes that didn't mean anything at all.

But my shoes were by the side of the stream.

One more day. One more day with Kit and then I'd do what I promised Patrick—I'd go to camp and follow the rules.

Mom and Patrick rushed to get ready while I tried to hide my bare feet under the table.

"Caleb," Mom said, "are you okay to get yourself out of the house and off to camp today? I'm going to give Patrick a lift to Dr. Edwards's office."

I nodded, trying hard not to smile into my Apple Jacks. "No problem."

Mom paused in front of the television, which was turned to the local news. "Hey, it's Mr. McDaniel!"

"Who's that?" I asked, midbite.

"One of my clients. He was just in for a cleaning last week. Quirky old man, collects everything you can imagine—pens with business logos, toy trucks, pencil sharpeners. He's most proud of his antique bottle collection, though."

My head jerked toward the television so fast something popped in my neck. "What?"

"Oh, this is terrible!" Mom clicked up the volume.

The newscaster, the same pretty lady who had talked about the dog, held a microphone under the mouth of an elderly man in a seersucker suit. They stood outside a falling-apart barn that looked horribly familiar. The old man was midsentence: ". . . store boxes of the old bottles out here, out of the way, like. I came in to get some of my favorites—old green and blue glass—all smashed. Boxes of 'em, just thrown here against the wall."

I couldn't tear my eyes from the screen. The newscaster pulled the mic back. "Do you have any idea who would do such a thing—any break-ins in the past?"

The old man shook his head. "No, never. I gotta think whoever done this ain't all right in the head."

"What makes you say that, Mr. McDaniel?" the newscaster asked.

"Well, they took a giant dump in the corner, didn't they?"

Patrick choked on his laugh, Mom gasped, and the newscaster pulled back the mic. "Back to you in the studio, Ron!" Mom clicked off the television.

"How bizarre," she said, and pulled her purse up her shoulder. No one looked at me. No one suspected me. I forced myself to breathe in and out. "I'll pick you both up here at about two o'clock—so keep an eye on the time and head home early, Caleb," Mom said. "Then I'll take you to get your tux fittings."

"Tux? What?" I asked.

Mom paused, looking at me like I had just asked if Patrick was polite or if water was wet. "Of course. For the fund-raiser."

"I thought it was a race?" I felt like I was testing out my voice, making it steady despite *another* news story about something horrible I had done.

"The race is Saturday," Patrick said. He was straightening his tie in the hall mirror. Yes, he actually wore ties to his internship. "Friday night is a black-tie event for sponsors."

"Do we *have* to go?" I asked. All I wanted to do ever again was stay put in the house.

"Of course we do," Mom said sharply. "Patrick is playing a concerto he wrote especially for the event."

"Of course he is," I echoed.

Mom kissed my forehead as she walked out the door. "Your brother has worked hard for this fund-raiser all summer; he even created a slideshow to play during his concerto. I can't wait to see it all come together." She paused and came back, kissing my head again. "Your forehead's a little hot. Are you okay?" Mom pressed her hand against my cheek.

"I'm fine," I said, shrugging her off. "Just thrilled about tux shopping, I guess."

Mom laughed. "Call me if you feel sick, okay?"

The moment the car pulled out of the driveway, I grabbed the blue serum bottle from under my bed. I buried it under a tree on my way to see Kit.

⸗⋙⋘⸗

I knew Kit was waiting on Mermaid Rock.

The crows told me.

They perched on either side of the stream, cawing and screeching. As I got closer, I saw them, swooping from one branch to the next, again and again, dipping lower and lower over where Kit sat huddled in the middle with her hands over her ears. I splashed across the stream, past my damp sneakers that were still waiting along the edge, and grabbed Kit's hand. Together, we ran back to her house, through the open door, past piles of trash and half-emptied boxes, past her mother asleep on the couch, up the staircase, and into the turret room at the top.

I looked around her room. The walls were covered with drawings, sketches on torn-out pages of old books. Drawings of birds. Of fairies flying over treetops. Of me, with water lapping over my ears and my eyes shut. "When did you do these?" I asked. They weren't little kid drawings or garbled messes like I would've done. They were perfect snapshots, done in pencil.

For the first time since I had met her, Kit looked embarrassed. Her cheeks were pink and she didn't seem to know what to do with her hands. She twisted them into the hem of her T-shirt. "I draw sometimes, at night." Kit touched the one of me. "It helps me remember."

Along the edge of the circular room was a pile of old books. I saw gaps where pages were missing. I felt a pang for the notebook I had made her, now shoved into a drawer of my desk. I should've given it to her. She shouldn't have had to draw on other people's stories like this.

"You're awesome," I said.

She smiled, more pink blossoming on her cheeks. "Grandmom and I used to draw a lot. I didn't think she'd mind if I used her books."

I looked around. Next to the pile of books were trash bags with clothes in them. One had clothes kind of folded (well, I'd consider them folded. Mom wouldn't). The other was jammed with what looked like dirty clothes. She didn't have a closet in the room. "I thought you said you slept here?" I didn't see a bed anywhere.

"Yeah," Kit said and pointed to a pile of blankets. "Right here. It's been too hot some nights, so I go to the porch. Grandmom said she used to sleep on the porch, too."

I nodded, like it was normal to not have a bed or a closet. I guessed for her, it was.

"About the bird," I started, "it's not your fault. You didn't know." And then I told her about what Derek said, about how the crows hold a grudge.

Kit shook her head. "No, it's not that. The fairies are mad at me. I shouldn't have returned their gift."

"Kit—" I shook my head, but she cut me off.

"Why is it so hard for you to believe?" she said, her crystal eyes wide. She closed her eyes as if thinking through where to begin. When she opened them again, they spilled over with tears. "I wish Grandmom were here. She'd tell you so you understood—everything. You'd believe her, I know you would, Caleb!"

I didn't say anything.

"Grandmom told me, Caleb, my whole life she told me about the fairies. And it was true. It *is* true. That's why Mama is the way she is. It's true. It's true!"

I thought about angels dancing on my fingertips. "Maybe it was just a story," I whispered.

"No!" Kit stomped her foot. "No." She turned from me, staring at the drawing of me in the stream. "I thought you were special, too, Caleb. I thought out of anyone, you'd understand!"

"Understand what?" I asked.

Kit turned then, her hands curled into fists. "What it's like! To know things no one else does. To be different!"

"I do understand," I said, "but this . . . this is crazy."

"Don't you say that!" Kit stomped her foot again. "Don't you say that word. It isn't." She rushed toward me, gripping my shoulders and looking me straight in the eye just like Mom had days before.

"Then what is it?" I asked. "What is it really?"

She told me, then, what her grandmother, the seer of the unknown, had told her. About how her mom had been beautiful, a perfect child. How special she had always been, right up until she ran off as a teenager. How a fairy must've fallen in love with her because one day she came back to Grandmom, with Kit growing in her belly and fairies only she could see in her eyes. How Grandmom told Kit they just had to keep her mom safe, how it wasn't her fault, how it was no one's fault. How Kit had nothing to fear from the fairies because she was one of them, how that protected her. But that Kit had to try every day to bring her mom back to make her theirs again, to convince her to take medicine from doctors that would block the fairies, talk her into finding work, and, most of all, to keep secret when Mama lost control, even if it meant being lonely or hungry or sad sometimes. It's what they had to do to keep Mama safe, Kit said. "I never told anyone else about it, ever," Kit said. "But when you gave me the book, when you appeared in the woods out of nowhere, I knew the fairies sent you. We're destined to be friends."

We were sitting with our backs to the side of the turret, seeing only sky and clouds in the windows all around us, like sitting on a cloud. She smiled and rested her head against my shoulder. My head swam, trying to make sense of everything she told me, trying to separate stories from truth, and I couldn't. I couldn't find the spot where one stopped and the other started. I closed my eyes and instead of clouds, I saw shadow parents.

"Do you believe now?" Kit asked.

I closed my eyes, remembering the first moment I saw Kit. Of course I believed her. I had known from that second that she was magical.

-»»».«««-

I stumbled across the stream, doubling back for my sneakers (again), that afternoon. We had spent all day in the turret, darting down the stairs to go to the bathroom. We shared my lunch, but I only ate half a sandwich. My stomach was all clenched up. Maybe it was because we were so high in the sky. I pretended not to notice how Kit stashed our leftovers under the blankets she slept on. I played music on my phone until the battery died a couple hours later and a few times we even danced ourselves silly, jumping around to the fast songs. Kit said nothing would wake up her mom when she was like that. Plus, she said, music was a kind of magic.

I ran back toward the park, past the shield in the hollow tree like usual, and darted to the sidewalk when the coast was clear. They must've been doing a craft or something else lame at the park because I couldn't hear any of the other campers as I headed home, even though I figured it was barely three o'clock.

And then, just before my house came into view, I remembered. It was like a puzzle piece fell from the sky and onto my head. The tux fitting. Mom was going to pick us up at two o'clock. Maybe it wasn't too late; my phone had died at about one. Maybe I only thought a couple hours had passed! My heart raced but my feet, they just stopped, as quick as if they landed in super glue, when I got outside my house.

Because there, on the porch, were baskets filled with construction paper cards. A half dozen Captain America and Avengers balloons were looped together. A giant GET WELL SOON banner lay abandoned on the grass. Sitting next to it was Shelly, looking bored and snooty and not at all surprised to see me.

"Wow, you're in trouble."

Just then, a high-pitched screechy voice yelled, "He hasn't been there for *how* long?"

Shelly leaned back on her elbows. "So much trouble."

CHAPTER FIFTEEN

Once again, I was sitting on the couch with angry-faced Mom and Dad across from me.

"I demand an explanation!" Mom yelled for the thousandth time.

I stared at my hands.

"Why weren't you at camp like you led all of us to believe?" Mom asked.

I shrugged.

Dad sighed. He did an exaggerated version of my shrug. "Sorry to inconvenience you. But it was kind of inconvenient to shell out a couple grand for a camp you've been to twice all summer. *Twice!*"

"It's not about the money as much as it is us not knowing what you're doing," Mom volleyed. "Where were you? What were you doing?"

Now I stared at a dark spot on the beige carpet. It kept jumping, or maybe that was just my head. It pounded with every breath I pushed in and out.

"Caleb," Mom said, softer now, "don't you understand that we *need* to know. You don't have the luxury of doing whatever you'd like. You have special concerns. *We* have special concerns regarding you."

"I'll do better," I said. "I'll go to camp tomorrow."

"Darn right you're going to camp!" Dad bellowed.

I stood, my legs wobbling. "I don't feel well. Can I go to bed?"

Dad crossed his arms. "Sit down. Your nap can wait."

I sat.

Mom didn't look up. "Do you have any idea what it was like for me just now? Wondering why you're late and then the camp counselor shows up with balloons—with get-well cards—wanting to let you know they've missed you so much."

I shook my head, now staring at the layer of dust on the coffee table.

"Of course not," Dad snapped. "You never think of anybody but yourself."

I stood again. "I really need to go to bed. I'm sorry."

"Sit down!" Mom and Dad yelled together.

I sat.

"I want to know exactly how you've been spending your days," Mom said. "I know it isn't here. Patrick told me he gets home before you or at the same time almost every day and it's clear no one's been there."

"I don't know, Mom," Patrick butted in from where he sat at the kitchen table. "It's not like I was searching for clues or anything. I guess he could've been here and then left just before I got home so it wouldn't look like anyone had been here."

"Is that what happened, Caleb?" Mom demanded. "Were you just staying at home all day? Why would you do that?"

Patrick cleared his throat. "Well, he is a lot older than most of the other kids at camp. There was only one other twelve-year-old and she's the counselor's cousin."

I stared at my shoelace.

"Is that it, Caleb?" Mom asked. "Are you embarrassed to be at camp?"

"Can I have a drink of water?" I asked instead of answering.

"Go to your room," Mom snapped. "Go to your room and don't come out until I tell you otherwise."

Hours later, Mom brought in a tray of food and left without saying anything. It was dark when I woke up, shrugged on my vest, and went through my nighttime meds. I clicked on *Captain America*. It was the scene where he got his shield for the first time.

I smiled, even though no one was there to see it. Here's the thing: While I sort of felt sick, I also felt really good. For the first time in a long time, I felt *good*. I wasn't carrying around a heavy secret. Mom

224

and Dad *knew* I hadn't been to camp. It was over.

Mom opened the door before I could wipe the smile off my face. She turned off the TV, unplugged it, and carried it from the room.

I stopped feeling so good after that.

※

Mom woke me the next morning by standing in the doorway and saying, "Get up."

She was still mad then.

I was a little dizzy as I got to the kitchen, and my head pounded, but no way was I going to complain to Mom. She had made a big production out of announcing that she had to take the day off work to get Patrick in to rent a tuxedo since we missed the appointment the night before. I didn't ask about my tux. I sort of guessed my invitation had been revoked.

"Crows are worked up today," Patrick said as we walked to Mom's car. Kit was waiting for me at Mermaid Rock, I knew. As the birds screeched, I wondered how long she'd wait for me there.

※

So if you skip camp for a couple months, leaving the other campers under the impression you're sick, and then a whole week of camp is spent making stupid get-well cards for you, no one is all that jazzed to see you upon your return.

Plus, it was the last week of camp, and just about everyone had a group. Four guys sat on top of a picnic table hashing it out about Pokémon cards they found in one their parents' basement. About a dozen kids played tag, the same guys going after the same girls each time. A few people did the craft—crocheting pot holders—with Ava in the center of the pavilion. Another trio played soccer. In fact, the only one *not* doing something with someone else was, of course, Shelly. She leaned against the wall of the pavilion, her feet up on a chair, reading comic books.

I sat on the other side of the pavilion and tried not to think about how long Kit had waited for me to show that morning, how much angrier than usual my dad was, and when my mom might smile at me again.

After lunch (I'm sure it was just a coincidence that Mom packed all the foods I don't like—ham and American with mustard, sour cream and onion chips, vanilla snack cakes, and soggy grapes), Ava told us all to change for the pool. I didn't bother, just slumped into the lounge chair by the water.

I couldn't stop shivering even though it was like ninety degrees out. I grabbed one of the beach towels off the rack and pulled it around me like the world's worst blanket. Here's the thing: by then, I knew I wasn't just nervous or guilty and that was what was making me wobbly and giving me a headache. I figured out I was actually sick. But it was such horrible timing. Would anyone at camp even believe

226

me if I was like, "Oh, hey, you know how I let you all think I was sick all summer? Now, I actually *am* sick." The last thing I needed was to bother Mom. So I tried to ignore it. Until I couldn't.

The football guys showed up, Brad at the helm, and dove into the pool, even though the lifeguards whistled at them and the splash shot chlorinated water up the noses of all the littler kids in the pool. I rolled onto my side away from them.

"Hey!" Jett shouted. "Brad, isn't that Caleb? I heard he was dying or something."

"Nope!" I heard Brad shout back from the other side of the pool. "Turns out he's just a liar."

"Ouch," Shelly said as she sat on the lounge chair next to me. She tossed a comic book onto the chair. "Finished this one. It's pretty good."

"Thanks," I muttered. I opened the book, but the words danced around the page. I was so, so cold. My teeth banged into each other.

"You don't look so good, Caleb," Shelly said.

"I-I'mmmm fine." My legs curled up toward my stomach as the coughing started. Hacks erupted out of me like lava. I couldn't stop it, couldn't sit up, couldn't do anything but cough.

"Ava!" Shelly screamed. "Ava!"

⇜⇝

Mom's car screeched into the parking lot a few minutes later.

Her face blurred in and out of focus in front of me, her hand scalded

227

me as she laid it across my forehead. "He's burning up," she said. "We need to get him to the hospital."

"Should I call nine-one-one?" someone—Ava—said behind her.

"It'll be faster for us to go straight there than to wait for an ambulance," Mom said.

And then I was in the air, lifted by two steady arms, one under my knees, the other under my arms. Patrick. When did he get strong enough to lift me up like that? "Thanks," I muttered.

"Don't mention it," he said back.

-꧁꧂꧁꧂-

Four days later, I heard Dr. Edwards talking to Mom and Dad just outside my hospital room. I kept my eyes closed and pretended to be sleeping.

"Frankly," Dr. Edwards said, "we're incredibly lucky he's never been this sick before. This is only the third time he's had pneumonia since he was diagnosed, which is remarkable."

"Lucky?" Dad snapped.

"Yes," Dr. Edwards said firmly, "very lucky. In no small part due to Steph's constant vigilance. But the truth is, despite all the advances we continue to make with CF, it's a progressive disease. I think it's time we start making some serious decisions."

"Like what?" Mom voiced my question.

"I never want to be this caught off guard by Caleb again. It's too challenging to bring his white blood cells back to an appropriate level from where they plummeted. I want him in for IV antibiotic infusions every four months, year round. He'll be admitted under a controlled environment, stick around for two weeks, and then we'll release him stronger and better able to fight infections before they settle."

I peeked through my lashes. Dad leaned against the doorway. "We're there already?"

Dr. Edwards said, "This isn't a bad thing, George. It's what he needs and where many, many of my patients have been for years before they reach his age. With any luck, that and Caleb's commitment to his physio care, we should be able to get to his twenties—maybe even through them—before he's on the transplant list."

The transplant list. As in a surgery to take out my crap lungs and put healthier lungs inside of me. And then I'd spend the rest of my life turning those healthy lungs into crap lungs. Lung transplants aren't a cure for CF. There isn't a cure for CF. *Yet,* I heard Dad's voice say in my head. He once held out hope like a ray of sunshine I was supposed to stretch toward that doctors would figure out a cure before I needed a double lung transplant—or worse.

"But he's almost thirteen," Mom said, and I didn't know if that meant she thought I was old or I was young.

No one said anything for a long moment. Dr. Edwards cleared his throat. "I'll leave you to discuss this."

I peeked again. Dad was still in the doorway. His face looked white, but maybe that was just the hospital lights. "I-I should—" And then his big hands were covering his face, his shoulders rocked back and forth, and my dad—

I squeezed my eyes shut and opened them again, sure I wasn't seeing what I was seeing. My dad was crying. That wasn't even right. He wasn't crying. He was *sobbing*. My dad was sobbing in the doorway.

Mom's birdlike hands darted toward him and back, toward him and back. They landed on his shoulders, and just like that, Dad fell against her. "I know," she cooed, just as she did when I was a kid crying over getting a shot. "I know."

"I don't want him to go through this," Dad said in heaving gulps. "I don't want this for him."

"I know," Mom whispered.

"I can't fix him, Steph. Why can't I fix him? I tried. But I failed again and again."

"You tried."

"But I can't fix him."

"Then just love him."

⟶››✦‹‹⟵

Two weeks later, I sat in a wheelchair.

Only it wasn't a wheelchair. I mean it was, but it didn't look like one. It looked like a race car, painted with a face in the front like the talking car from that Pixar movie. Like having a wheelchair painted with a character will totally make up for the whole being in a wheelchair part. Only I was almost thirteen, and I would have much preferred a real no-thrills gray wheelchair to make my exit after two weeks in the hospital. Instead, Mom was taking endless pictures of me being pushed down the hall by Dad in a red race car wheelchair with a half dozen balloons tied to the handles and the teddy bear my grandma had sent. When I was totally out of it I had apparently cuddled with it in my sleep. Mom had pictures of that, too, which, in totally awesome news, she had posted to social media, kick-starting a prayer chain for me.

Once in the middle of those two weeks, I woke up and thought I saw angels dancing at the tips of Derek's fingers as he knelt beside my bed. I didn't say anything, though. Even in my delirium, I realized talking about seeing angels would only serve to freak Mom out to brand-new levels of freak-out-dom.

My thoughts ran a million miles per hour, and I didn't think any of that had to do with my race car wheelchair. It was like I just woke up after hibernation or something. My mind was suddenly super alert, thinking through and piecing together everything I missed, even though my body worked slowly and deliberately. I had lost weight in the hospital, something that really worried Mom, who kept talking about taking me home and "fattening me up."

Things that I slept through or around during the previous two weeks kept popping into my mind like someone cut up comic book squares and I had to put them back in order, panel by panel, until I made an entire strip.

First strip, panel one: Perfect Patrick. Mom downloaded a bunch of old home movies to her iPad and brought them in for me to watch. She crawled into the bed with me, watching over my shoulder. The one that kept running in my mind now was me, about a year old, sitting in a high chair. I had a toy—a truck, I think—and kept throwing it on the ground. Every time I did, Patrick, who was about six, picked it up and put it back on my tray. Again and again, I threw it, laughing with a two-toothed grin right into the camera. Again and again, Patrick picked it up and put it back, until he was crying as loud as I laughed. Off camera, Dad said, "Why don't you just leave it on the ground?" to Patrick. Mom, who had been filming laughed, "Patrick, it's okay! Just leave it." But Patrick didn't. He wouldn't.

Panel two: Patrick pushing his chair all the way in the far corner of the room, never looking up once but never leaving, either, when Mom or Dad couldn't be there.

Panel three: Patrick coming by in his tuxedo after the fundraiser. He grinned at Mom as he walked in and started to tell her about the event I made her miss, but then I started to cough and my oxygen levels dipped and alarms started buzzing, and soon all I could see were doctors and Mom's worried face.

Second strip: Friends I didn't deserve. Panel one: Brad standing next to the bed, arms crossed and face set. "I hope you feel better soon," he said, and left before I could answer.

Panel two: Shelly Markel, storming in with armloads of comic books. She dumped them all on my bed and loaded the *Avengers* DVD into the hospital room player. Without saying hello or asking me how I was doing or anything else, she pulled up the chair beside my bed, crossed her ankles on the edge of it, and hit play on the remote. "Hulk is the absolute worst Avenger," she said, which of course led to us fighting for the best half hour of the entire hospital stay.

"You know I used to wish I was in the hospital. Isn't that stupid?" Shelly shuddered.

"They're not so bad," I said. "Aside from the bad food, stiff beds, weird smells, and, you know, the needles and stuff." Shelly stared out the window at the parking lot. "And the terrible views."

"I know it's stupid," she whispered, "but I used to be so jealous of you."

"Yeah," I snorted. "Living it up over here."

Her eyes slid toward mine and I couldn't smile anymore. "Everyone tries so hard to be good to you, to be your friend, even when you're not ... not ..."

"Not worth it?" I finished.

"No!" Shelly stood, shaking her head, then sank back in her seat. "No, you're worth it. I just don't get why I'm—"

Silence can be louder than a thousand crows.

My voice was too loud when I spoke because of that. "Maybe we could both try being a little more—"

"You know," Shelly interrupted, plucking the comic book back off the edge of my bed, "why do you like Captain America so much?"

"Because he was born sick and weak, but became strong."

Shelly replied without a second's hesitation, "No, he was born strong. His body was weak." Cue doctor coming in and taking me for another chest X-ray.

Panel three would be a completely black square. That one was for Kit, who had no way of knowing where I was or why I had left.

Panel four: People I didn't deserve. And it would show my family, surrounding me now around my stupid baby race car wheelchair.

Derek put his hand under my elbow when we got to the parking lot. "Thanks," I said as he helped me into the backseat. "I can actually walk, though."

"Your mom says you're supposed to take it easy, so you'll be taking it easy," he said back with a smile. "But I'm glad to see you out of that place."

"You and me both," I replied, and pushed the race car wheelchair back with my foot.

Derek's windows were down so I heard Mom and Dad as they stood in front of the car. Dad said, "I'll follow you home."

"That won't be necessary," Mom said. "Derek's here. He'll help me get Caleb into the house."

"I can walk!" I shouted from the backseat. They both ignored me.

"I can—" Dad started.

"No," Mom said, her voice firm. "We have it from here. You can go to your home."

⟶≫≫ ⟪⟪⟵

Mom stayed home with me the next two days, but finally she relaxed as she realized I really was getting stronger.

And I was. I coughed up a ton of phlegm and started to feel like myself. I was home for four days before I had a chance to go see Kit.

Mom fell asleep on the couch—she had been sleeping so lightly that every time I rolled over at night, she shouted, "Are you okay?" And Patrick was back in his room playing his violin. Lately he'd been doing that for hour-long or more stretches. It got so I had a hard time falling asleep without the music.

I knew it was wrong to sneak out when I had just made a billion promises to get my act together, but I had to see Kit.

I couldn't leave that square empty. I had to tell her what happened. I was going to tell her the truth, all of it. I was going to tell her I had CF and everything that meant. Mostly, I was going to tell her that it meant I couldn't be like her—I couldn't listen to what the lines in my palm meant or see meaning in a bird left alone or take something just because the person who had it didn't appreciate it. I couldn't do whatever I wanted.

235

And there was more. I was going to tell her she needed help, too, and she should talk to a grown-up. I was going to tell her she was too old for fairy tales.

I had it all planned out, what I was going to say.

I was going to be back before Mom ever woke up or Patrick stopped playing his violin.

I was going to be right back. That's even what I wrote on the note I propped up on the table next to the couch, just in case.

I'll be right back.

CHAPTER SIXTEEN

The crows were silent as I plowed down the path toward Mermaid Rock. I figured that meant I'd have to find Kit at her house and was so surprised to see her sitting there on the rock, sun falling across her shoulders and making another halo over her dark hair, that I gasped.

If she was as surprised to see me as I was her, Kit didn't show it. She merely glanced over at me and quickly looked back at her book.

I plunged ahead, kicking off my shoes and crossing the stream. It must've rained a lot while I was gone; the water lapped at my calves. I told myself that was why it was so hard to cross the water, not that I already was tired from the short walk. I pulled myself onto the rock and didn't speak, just waited for my breathing to go back to normal.

"The crows stopped," I said.

Kit didn't look up from her book. "They moved away. Once the baby started to fly, they took off."

I settled beside her, wondering where to begin.

"Where've you been?" Kit didn't look up from the book. She had lost weight, too. Her arms looked like pale twigs. Sitting next to her, I noticed something else. She smelled odd, like clothes left in the washing machine too long before drying. There were dark circles under her eyes. How many days had her mom traded for tomorrows while I was gone?

"I've been sick," I told her. "Kit, there's something I haven't told you. Something you need to know about me."

Kit looked up then and her crystal eyes never left mine the whole time I told her about cystic fibrosis—that it meant my lungs functioned differently. That it was why I had to go to the bathroom so often and eat so much. That it was why I had to go to the hospital and take a lot of medicine. That it meant unless they could find a cure, I'd probably never be an old man. That it was why I couldn't always do what I wanted but also why I had to make every day mine.

"It's something I was born with," I finished. "They didn't know right away—no one in our family has had it for generations—but when I started to get sick, they figured it out."

At this, Kit's mouth popped open. "How old were you when you started to get sick?"

I shrugged. "I don't know exactly. I was diagnosed when I was two, though."

"Cystic fibrosis," Kit whispered. She chewed her lip. "But what if it's not?"

I tilted my head. "What if what's not?"

"What if"—Kit's eyes grew story-size—"that's not what happened at all." She pointed to the book in her hand, the book I had stolen from Mom to give to her. "This book is full of stories about totally healthy babies becoming sick. About parents doing everything they can to make them well and never being able to do it. The reason: They're not babies at all! They're changelings."

"What?"

"Changelings," Kit said. She flipped open the book to a drawing of a screaming, skinny, pale baby and read aloud: *"Occasionally a fairy child is swapped for a human one, particularly if the human child is as beautiful as a fairy child and lives near an enchanted forest."* Kit looked around at the stream and trees, then back to the book. *"The fairies typically just wish to play with the human child for a bit of fun and intend to swap back the children in due course. However, fairy time is different than human time. Sometimes so much human time passes that the fairy child forgets its fay nature and begins to believe he is human."*

"Kit," I interrupted, my heart pounding, "I really have to get back. I don't think—"

"Just wait!" Kit cried. She continued, *"Fairies cannot live with humans without feeling ill effects. Often changeling children will be*

misdiagnosed as having genetic diseases from birth, although symp-
toms don't arise until they've lived amongst humans for years. Until
then, the child, almost always pale with huge eyes,—Caleb!—*will be the*
picture of health."

"Kit, it's just a story—"

But Kit raised her voice: *"To be healthy again, even if he wishes*
to remain amongst his human family, he must track down his true fay
parents. A kiss from them every two decades will fortify his nature so he
can continue his parallel life." She slammed shut the book. "That's it,
Caleb!"

"No." I shook my head. "No, that's not it. That's not me. It's just
a story!"

"Open your eyes! It all fits." Kit jumped down into the stream and
threw her arms wide. "All of it! *Think*. You didn't intend to find me
that day you were going for a walk. And I had never been here before
that very day. Yet we found each other. In this whole forest, *we found*
each other! I know a lot about the fay, and you have this book." She
jabbed her thumb to where the book perched on the rock beside me.

"That's a coincidence," I whispered.

Kit shook her head. "You know it's not! Destiny brought us
together. We were supposed to find each other. You needed me to
lead you to the fay, to cure you before you get too sick! And I needed
you to—"

"To what?" I whispered.

"To be my friend!" she shouted. "To be my friend even if you saw Mama. To be my friend and to believe me, to believe the stories as much as me." She grabbed my arm and yanked so I slid down into the water, too. She turned toward the woods. "Let's go!"

I pulled back my hand. "It's just a story, Kit. They're all just stories."

"No!" she yelled in my face. "No!"

"I'm sick. It's all right. Maybe they'll find a cure. I mean, I'm better than I was." I shoved my hands in my pockets and glanced toward the trail leading back home. Was Mom still asleep? "I'm tired and maybe my words aren't coming out right, but Kit . . ." I closed my eyes, thought of angels dancing on fingertips just to keep a child sitting still. "Maybe your grandmom wasn't a seer. Maybe she just needed to tell you a story because it was easier than telling you your mom was sick. Maybe whoever came up with changeling myths did it because it's easier than dealing with the fact that some kids get handed a raw deal."

"No." Kit grit her teeth. She grabbed my arm again. "The book says fay leave trails near hollow trees or grassy knolls. We just need to find the right one." Kit yanked on my arm harder, making me stumble forward so my knees slammed down into the water. Man, it was cold.

"You're not sick. You're not," she said, and I heard the tears in her voice.

"Kit." I pushed myself back up on wobbling legs. I couldn't say more than her name, though, without pausing to take another breath. The water was so chilly, yet a cold sweat broke out across my face. I tried to slow down my breathing, but my shoulders tightened, and I could hardly move my neck. I coughed, not even bothering to bend my neck and cough into my elbow. My neck was so stiff I could barely move it. "Kit—no—"

"You're not sick!" she yelled, but she already was a yard away, stomping to the side of the stream and scanning the woods. She dried her face angrily with her palms. "We just need to find the right place. They *owe* us, Caleb. They *owe me*!"

I turned back to the rock, leaning against it while trying to find space to breathe between hacking coughs. I was coughing so much, so fast, that black dots bloomed behind my eyes. "Kit—"

"I'll find it myself if I have to," Kit cried without turning around. "I'll fix this!"

"*Kit* . . ." Everything went black as I fell into the water.

→≫≫·≪≪←

"Kit?"

"Caleb?" I opened my eyes, expecting to see Kit shining in the sunlight. Instead, Mom's red-rimmed eyes stared back. She brushed back my hair from my face. "You're back with us." She kissed my forehead and I smelled the coffee she must've been drinking.

"You look awful," I croaked. My throat was dry and cold, probably from the oxygen being pumped through the tubes in my nostrils.

Mom laughed. "You should see yourself." I closed my eyes when she started to cry.

⤳⟫⟫⟫⟪⟪⟪⤶

The next time I woke up, music was playing.

Patrick stood facing the window and its view of the hospital parking lot, sawing at his violin. The song was one I hadn't heard before. It was beautiful but hideous. A newly hatched–bird song. I didn't like the way it made me feel. Like I was hearing my worst thoughts woven together and laid out for everyone to see. "Do you like it?" Patrick asked. I hadn't realized he was watching me.

I shook my head, but said, "Yes."

Patrick laughed. "Me too. I wrote it for the fund-raiser."

I pulled myself up on my elbows. "Where are Mom and Dad?"

"They're meeting with the doctor. It doesn't look like your pneumonia is any worse. I mean, it's still a problem, but they think you had a massive panic attack when you started coughing."

I shook my head again. "No, I was sick."

Patrick nodded. "Right. Like I said, massive panic attack." He put the violin back into the hard black case. "So I was right about you having a girlfriend. Just wrong about which one."

"What happened?" I ask. "I only remember falling."

"That girl, Kit, she saw you fall. She pulled you over to the shore.

243

I don't know how. She's probably the only person skinnier than you. Anyway, she pulled you to the shore and came barreling through the woods, screaming that you needed help. Mom heard her and came running. You've got to stop sneaking off like that."

"Don't worry," I said, and rubbed my palms into my eyes. "I won't do it again."

"I don't need to worry," Patrick said. "Mom's putting an alarm system on your windows and the doors."

"Seriously? Geez! She's overreacting!"

"It was Dad's idea," Patrick said.

For a few seconds, I just listened to Patrick pack up his violin. He did so deliberately, wiping down the shiny wood and laying it so it was cradled in the blue velvet case. "What was that song called? The one you just played," I finally asked.

Patrick's ears turned red. "'Caleb.'"

I stifled a groan but fell back against the bed. Once again Perfect Patrick does something noble.

"Don't worry," Patrick said, his voice cold. "No one you know heard it. Mom and Dad were at the hospital with you during the fund-raiser."

"Like I did that on purpose." I rolled onto my side, away from him. I guessed now Patrick would just have to show them how perfect he was by winning yet another race, getting another scholarship, or kicking butt in whatever it was he'd try next to show me up. Perfect

Patrick, at it again. He couldn't even leave CF to me.

"Do you know what it's like," Patrick said so softly I barely heard him, "to be your brother?"

I snorted. "Yeah, it must be *so hard* to outshine me in absolutely everything. Even breathing."

"Yeah." Patrick laughed, but it was brittle. "It is. It is crazy hard. All they want, all they've ever wanted from the time you were diagnosed, is for you to live. Live. That's all you have to do to be a success. Me? I've got to show them constantly that I'm here, too. I've got to prove that when—I mean, if . . ."

"Go ahead!" I shouted. And then immediately coughed. "Say it. When I *die*."

"When you die," Patrick repeated, his voice hollow, "I have to be as good as two sons."

❧

Mom came into the room a minute after Patrick stormed off. Too soon.

"Patrick?" I heard her say from the hall outside my room. "Are you okay? What's wrong?"

"He's awake," Patrick replied. In a moment, Mom was by my side, whatever she had seen in Patrick forgotten.

She breathed out long and gentle when I smiled at her, but she didn't smile back. She held the *World of Faerie* book. When Kit had gotten me help, she left the book behind, too. "When you're ready, Caleb, I have a lot of questions."

I pushed myself up on my pillows. "Mom," I said, "can I talk to you about Kit?" My mind, which had been sticky as chewed-up gum before—holding on to every single thought about Patrick, Brad, Shelly, Dad, Mom, camp, and lungs—suddenly focused.

I opened my mouth and I shattered Kit's life as surely as if I threw it against that barn door.

CHAPTER SEVENTEEN

When I finished telling Mom everything, she left the room. A little later she came back with a stranger. "Caleb, this is Ms. Grimes. She wants to talk to you about what you told me." Mom glanced from me to the woman. She was young, maybe in her midtwenties, with red lipstick and eyes lined in black. Her hair was curly and when she took off her jacket and pulled up a chair to sit next to me, I saw angel wings tattooed on her shoulders.

"You can call me Jess," she said as she sat down. I saw a badge clipped to her jacket pocket and my heart got thumpy again.

"Are you a police officer?" I asked.

Jess paused. "No. I work for the government, though. Do you need a police officer?"

"It's just—I committed a crime."

Jess nodded and her red lips twitched. "Your mom mentioned that. You set loose a dog, right? I did a little digging there. One of my friends is an animal control officer. That dog has been found. Turns out he's mostly wolf. They found a place for him in a sanctuary a few hours from here."

"He?" I repeated.

Jess nodded. "He's quite happy, from what I understand. They named him Ralph. And his former owner is facing a hefty fine for buying a wild animal." She shifted in the plastic chair. "I know about the barn, too. Mr. McDaniel does not plan to press charges. I think your mom had something to do with that."

"If Mom told you everything already, why do you need hear it from me?" I asked.

Mom pulled her purse up her arm. "I'm going to grab a cup of coffee. Jess, would you like any?"

"Yeah," she said. "That'd be great."

"Cream and sugar?" Mom asked.

"Nope. Black as my soul." Mom didn't laugh, but I did. Jess winked at me as Mom left the room. "I work with an agency that looks out for kids. If they're in trouble or need help, I help them find what they need. I need you to tell me what's going on with your friend so I know how to help her."

"Are you going to take Kit from her mom?"

Jess folded her hands on her lap. "If that's what she needs in order to be safe, and for her mom to get the help *she* needs, then yes. But maybe you could tell me a little about what you shared with your mom and then we'll decide what to do?"

"Can I ask you something first?"

"Of course." Jess smiled. Her front tooth bent over the one beside it. I liked that about her.

"Do you believe in fairy tales?"

Jess glanced out the window for a second. "As in everyone gets a happily ever after? And maybe there are guardians, fairy godmothers or whatever, out there, waiting for the perfect moment to appear and fix everything?"

I nodded.

"No," she answered. "I don't. I think we have to sometimes fight to get what we need. And what we need isn't always what we want. Sometimes getting what we need—what we see others need, too—hurts."

I didn't speak for a moment. "I don't know where to start."

"Start at the beginning," Jess said. "What's the first thing you remember about Kit?"

I swallowed, thinking about the trees I saw growing apart from each other the day I met Kit. About how that meant they were friends. "Kit says it was destiny that we met, but I was just going for a walk."

I got out of the hospital two days later. Mom made me stay in bed for another two days after that, even though I felt fine.

Jess stopped by the house and told us she had followed up with Kit. She said what she found out backed up what I had told her. Kit's mom wasn't capable of taking care of her. Kit sometimes went days without eating or having a safe place to sleep. Jess said Kit had been in danger, and I knew deep inside that falling out of the tree hadn't been what bruised her face. Now Kit lived in a new town, with an older couple who always wanted to have a daughter. "She's with a very kind family," Jess said. "She gets to be a kid."

"She hates me, doesn't she?" I said.

Jess squeezed my hand. "Someday she'll understand."

I shook my head. She wouldn't understand. She'd never understand. "Are there trees at her new house?"

Jess just smiled.

I held out the notebook I had made for Kit, the one with the bad painting of the crow and all the empty pages. "Will you give her this from me?" Jess said she would try.

On the third day, I told Mom I was going to Mermaid Rock. Just like that. I said, "I'm going to Mermaid Rock."

Mom was sitting with Derek on the couch. Both of them looked at me for a long time. "She's not there, Caleb," Mom said. Even though she stayed seated, even though Derek squeezed her shoulder, Mom's hands rose like she wanted to pull me toward her.

I stepped back. "I know. I just want to go there."

Mom nodded. Her hands dropped. "Take your phone."

I went back to my room to grab my phone. Derek stood by the front door as I made my way toward it. "Do you want any company?" he asked.

I shook my head and pushed past him. But I turned, halfway out the door. "Do you really think trees can be friends?"

Derek nodded, looking down at his shoes. "I do."

"Do you think it hurts to grow apart? When they're friends, I mean."

Derek did look up then. He nodded again. "I'm sure it does."

I thought about that now as I walked back to our rock. I rubbed at the aching in my chest, telling myself the pain was okay. Maybe someday I'd hear from Kit again. Maybe not.

On the way to the rock, I dug up the blue serum bottle. I grabbed the bark shield, too. At the stream's edge, I kicked off my shoes. The woods were so quiet, the water so cold. I climbed the rock and stood upon it.

Kit wasn't here, so I talked to the trees.

"You were right," I said, my voice echoing through the woods. "You were right. You said we were destined to be friends. You said everything would change because of it. You were right." I threw back my head and shouted it. "You were right!"

A single crow swooped overhead. I left the bottle and the shield on the rock as I slid off. The rock seemed so much smaller without her on it. Even though I wanted to, I didn't look back at the rock to see if the gift was accepted.

When I got back to the trail, Patrick was there. For a second—just a second—a flash of resentment went through me. "Hey, Patrick," I said instead of yelling at him.

"This is where you've been hanging out?"

"Yeah." I picked up a rock and skipped it across the stream. It bounced four times. Soon Patrick picked up one, too. His only skipped once and fell in.

"You've been a real jerk," Patrick muttered as he threw another stone. This one landed with a plunk.

"I know." I threw another stone. Seven skips. Then I shoved my hands in my pockets and forced words thicker than mud to come up through my mouth. "I'm sorry. I . . . I think sometimes it's easier to hate you than it is to hate all the things you get to do and I don't."

Patrick swallowed, his throat bobbing up and down. "Sometimes I do things just because you can't." He didn't look at me, just stared across the stream. "Can you show me how to skip rocks?"

So I did. I think he probably already knew how, but it was cool to teach him anyway.

Mom drove me to school the next day even though I usually took the bus. She waited in the car, watching me, as I walked into the building. She'd become a bit suspicious.

This year, we had to switch rooms for each class. Right before lunch, I had art class. We could draw whatever we wanted. I painted a blackbird. It still looked more like a blob than a bird, but I kind of liked it. The art room was on the other side of the building from the nurse's office, where I had to stop for Creon, so instead of being first for lunch like I had been the year before, I was last.

I'd like to say the whole cafeteria quieted as I walked in, waiting to see where I'd sit, but the truth is, no one seemed to notice. All the seats at Brad's table were taken, but I wouldn't have sat there if that were different. Brad had nodded when we passed in the hall earlier, but I could tell things were never going to be the same. Sometimes friends grow apart.

"Mind if I sit down?" I asked, standing just beside Shelly. I had to repeat it, since she had in earbuds and was listening to music.

She raised an eyebrow. "It's a free country," she said, and kicked a chair back a little for me to sit.

"Did you hear Black Widow's getting her own movie?" I asked as I unpacked my lunch box.

"'Bout time," Shelly said.

When the bell rang twenty minutes later, we were still debating whether Captain America should've risked everything for Bucky.

"Can I ask you something?" Shelly said.

"It's a free country."

She rolled her eyes. Hers were brown, like chocolate. Like mine. "Why'd you sit with me?" Shelly stared hard at her tray, her ears red. "If you're here to make fun of me . . ."

"No!" I said quickly. "It's not that at all. It's just . . . we both could use a friend, I think."

"No one put you up to this?" Shelly crossed her arms.

"Nah, I wouldn't do that." I smiled, thinking of Kit. "Besides, I do what I want."

(Plus, Patrick was right. Shelly was sort of cute.)

ACKNOWLEDGMENTS

Thank you doesn't begin to encompass the gratitude I have to those who opened their hearts and shared their experiences of living with cystic fibrosis. Many thanks especially to William Marler, an award-winning filmmaker and all-around great person. Will spreads awareness of cystic fibrosis through his podcast, *Straight from the Lungs*. Be sure to check it out! It's an honor to be part of it and an even greater honor to be his friend.

Thank you also to Charlee Peters and her son, Jack Shorter. Jack, who is about the same age as my son, is the epitome of optimism, focusing on the bright side whenever and however possible. His mom, Charlee, inspires me with her courage and strength.

I loved getting to know Rab of rmalikreports.wordpress.com. Thank you for sharing your experiences.

Caleb and Kit wouldn't have been the same without the insight they provided.

I wanted to write a book about friendship, about how sometimes being a good friend means you have to allow the other person to grow in a different direction. And I also wanted to write a book about a character who happens to have cystic fibrosis. Why? Because many children do.

But something happened as I wrote Caleb, as he began to grow and become real in my mind. Sharing his story became difficult. I didn't want him to be facing this reality. Thank you to my wonderful friend Cecy Robson, who sensed this when I floated the idea of changing the story from first to third person. "Knock it off," she told me. "If it scares you, if it's hard, it's important." As always, you were right.

Much love and gratitude to my incredible agent, Nicole Resciniti. You push me to dig deeper, celebrate the result, and then set a new challenge. Where would I be without you? I shudder to think. And to editor extraordinaires Julie Matysik and Adrienne Szpyrka—where do I begin? Having you in my corner means the world to me.

To my family, thank you doesn't cut it. Not for the days of pelting you with facts about crows and trees. Not for the playlists of songs that "Caleb would love" or that are "so, so Kit" that I made you listen to again and again. Not for blanking out in the middle of a conversation and running upstairs to scribble down a new idea. And not for blanking out through *entire* conversations, stuck in their world. But thank you is all I've got.

Finally, to Maura. You once told me, "You never know how strong you can be until you have to be for your child." And you are unbelievably strong. But you're also so much more. You're radiant, and my life is better because you're in it. Thank you also to Joey, the toughest little fighter I've ever known.